The Fire

"I can save us both," he said frantically. "A hundred feet inside and the smoke won't kill us."

She stopped him. "I can't move. It hurts too much."

He wept. "But I can't leave you! Jessa! You've got to try!"

She shook her head sadly. "No, I'll stay here. I have to stay here. Everything will be OK."

He understood that she couldn't move if she wanted to. Since he wouldn't leave her, there was nothing more to discuss. Smoke filled the tunnel like fog descending. Mark stretched out and lay down beside her. The flames could not touch them, but the superheated air would kill them just the same. Every inhalation was thick with gas. But through it all Jessa shivered and never lost her peaceful smile. It was one more mystery that he would never understand about her.

"This was meant to happen," she said.

It was the last words he heard.

The fire came near. The Magic Fire.

Books by Christopher Pike

CHAIN LETTER 2: THE ANCIENT EVIL
FINAL FRIENDS #1: THE PARTY
FINAL FRIENDS #2: THE DANCE
FINAL FRIENDS #3: THE GRADUATION
THE LAST VAMPIRE
THE LAST VAMPIRE 2: BLACK BLOOD
THE LAST VAMPIRE 3: RED DICE
THE LAST VAMPIRE 4: PHANTOM
THE LAST VAMPIRE 5: EVIL THIRST
THE LAST VAMPIRE 6: CREATURES OF FOREVER
THE LAST VAMPIRE COLLECTOR'S EDITION, VOLUME 1
THE LAST VAMPIRE COLLECTOR'S EDITION, VOLUME 2
REMEMBER ME
REMEMBER ME 2: THE RETURN
REMEMBER ME 3: THE LAST STORY
TALES OF TERROR #1
TALES OF TERROR #2

BURY ME DEEP
DIE SOFTLY
THE ETERNAL ENEMY
EXECUTION OF INNOCENCE
FALL INTO DARKNESS
GIMME A KISS
THE HOLLOW SKULL
THE IMMORTAL
LAST ACT
THE LOST MIND
MAGIC FIRE
MASTER OF MURDER
THE MIDNIGHT CLUB

MONSTER
ROAD TO NOWHERE
SCAVENGER HUNT
SEE YOU LATER
SPELLBOUND
THE STAR GROUP
THE STARLIGHT CRYSTAL
THE TACHYON WEB
THE VISITOR
WHISPER OF DEATH
THE WICKED HEART
WITCH

Available from ARCHWAY Paperbacks

Christopher Pike

Magic Fire

AN ARCHWAY PAPERBACK
Published by POCKET BOOKS
New York London Toronto Sydney Tokyo Singapore

This book is a work of fiction. Names, characters, places and incidents are products of the author's imagination or are used fictitiously. Any resemblance to actual events or locales or persons, living or dead, is entirely coincidental.

AN ARCHWAY PAPERBACK *Original*

An Archway Paperback published by
POCKET BOOKS, a division of Simon & Schuster Inc.
1230 Avenue of the Americas, New York, NY 10020

Copyright © 1999 by Christopher Pike

ISBN: 0-671-02057-9

First Archway Paperback printing June 1999

10 9 8 7 6 5 4 3 2 1

AN ARCHWAY PAPERBACK and colophon are registered trademarks of Simon & Schuster Inc.

Cover art by Franco Accornero

Printed in the U.S.A.

For the cold and beautiful
Susan Smyth

Magic Fire

1

Mark Charm sat in the audience and thought of love and fire. Jessa Welling had that effect on him; she cooled his longing and fanned his lust. If there was a perfect image for what was desirable in the world, she would be it. Especially on the stage, starring in *The Season of the Witch*—and particularly tonight, when so much in his life seemed so wrong. Sitting in the dark, in the third row, and watching Jessa cast her cunning spells on unsuspecting heroes and villains, Mark knew that he would give this life and his next for just one night with Jessa.

"And who are you?" Jessa's character, Ebo, asked a lost minstrel who had had the bad luck to stumble into her secret cave. "What is thy name? Thy place of birth? And what is thy deepest desire? Speak! Before I anger and burn you with a touch."

Jessa touched Speen, David Simmons's character, as she pronounced her threat. Mark thought of
Romeo and Juliet as she caressed Speen's cheek
with a gloved hand. Mark wished that he were a
hand upon that glove. Actually, he wished he were
David Simmons, handsome and confident enough
to star opposite Jessa.

"I am a mere mortal, lost in an illusion from
which there is no escape," Speen replied. "I have
come to you for truth and wisdom."

"Truth and wisdom!" Ebo said with a laugh.
"You will find neither here. You have entered a
realm of shadows, where only death can show you
light." She continued to stroke his cheek lovingly
and spoke softly. "Shall I show you this light now?
Or would you prefer to wait?"

Mark was tired of waiting. He had been trying to
summon the courage to speak to Jessa since the
first day of school eight weeks ago. Tonight he was
going to do it. Just walk up to her, after the play,
strike up a conversation, and ask her out. Jessa was
new to Zale High, a senior transfer from a prep
school back East, and Mark knew she would not
last long as a single white female in the school's
hormone jungle. She was not only pretty, but also
had talent, and Mark decided she must not be
human.

Yet, in reality, she was not a classic knockout,
but Mark could appreciate that fact and still maintain his steady state of crush. Jessa had short dark

hair and her face was pale, which made her large red lips almost vampirish. Her eyes were gray—up close slightly dazed looking—and she had a bad habit of chewing gum. She was not tall, nor exceptionally curvy, yet she was sexy. Perhaps it was because of her silence, her still presence, the way she could walk right by a person on a hot day and make that person feel the brush of a cool breeze. No question, she was a natural actress, and when she was onstage every eye was on her and her alone. Her soft voice projected like mental telepathy. Mark often heard her as he fell asleep at night, saying his name over and over.

Of course Mark knew that he had Jessa on a pedestal. She was a girl, mortal and flawed, and if she said no to him he would be crushed but he would get over it. He was intense by nature, obsessive at times, capable of major mood swings. Still, he did not see himself as unstable because he always knew when he was acting wild. But he was counting on getting to know her, more than he wanted to admit to himself. He had dated the last couple of years, but had never had anything approaching a girlfriend.

Yet Mark was by no means the class nerd, although he was smart and relatively shy. He was an excellent tennis player, number one in the league, and also an avid surfer. The outdoor exercise had built him a lanky, muscular body. His brown hair showed streaks of blond from being overexposed to the sun. With intense dark eyes, and a habit of falling into reflective silence while others babbled senselessly, he possessed his own quiet allure, a mystery that more than a few girls at Zale High found seductive. However, Mark was only vaguely aware of this private fan club. To go up to Jessa and ask her out was going to take the most nerve of his life.

Still, he vowed he would do it. Tonight.

Somehow, somewhere, he felt a clock ticking.

It was as if the sands of time were pouring over his heart.

The play went on, through three violent acts. The season of the witch finally came to a close as Ebo became the victim of one of her own curses. Ebo, who was now loved by Speen, died in his arms. He ended his life by jumping onto the funeral pyre he had built to consume Ebo's remains. Justice was served but at a bitter price. Ebo had not been a kind character and Mark felt that rather fitting because Jessa was no sweetheart either. The way she sauntered around campus demonstrated she had an attitude. But he, like Speen, was willing to endure it to be close to her. As the curtain fell after the final bow—accompanied by loud cheering—Mark was quickly on his feet and heading backstage.

He plunged into chaos. This was the last night of the play—Mark had seen it four times—and this final performance had been exceptional, which the

actors knew. The drama teacher, small and lump-
ish Ms. Chort, plowed the narrow halls behind the
stage issuing congratulations and high-pitched gig-
gles. All the actors were hugging and kissing and
acting as if heaven had finally opened above a dark
world. But Mark could not find Jessa and worried
she was already in the dressing room and very
possibly off limits. He knew she owned a car and
would probably be driving herself home.

Still, he had made a vow to himself and forced
himself to approach her dressing room door, located at the far end of the hall. Doubt dogged his
steps as the din from the others receded. He
knocked so softly he was sure she would not have
been able to hear. Yet her voice called out to come
in. God, she was asking for him, heart failure was
just over the threshold. He opened the door, stepped
inside, and closed the door behind him.

She was sitting with her back to him, in front of a
large makeup mirror. The mirror reflected a blank
wall, so he doubted she could see who was with her.
She dabbed at her eyes with a white cotton ball,
removing a layer of red powder. She was out of her
black robe and now sat scantily clad in a thin white
slip, her skin as soft as cream. Mark felt shame and
excitement, and as he cleared his throat to speak,
he almost choked on his tonsils.

"Am I disturbing you?" he asked.

She changed her angle to see him in the mirror,
but did not turn around.

"Who are you?" she asked.

"Mark Charm." He fidgeted. "I wanted to tell you how much I liked your performance."

"Thanks." She gestured casually toward a chair. "Have a seat."

"I can come back," he offered.

"No problem." She finally turned, without bothering to cover her breasts. Not that he could see them completely, but a lot was visible. The contours of her nipples poked through the fine material. She stared at him for a moment before slowly smiling and speaking, "I know you."

He sat with an audible thump. He didn't know where to put his hands, what to do with them. Finally he decided to leave them attached to the end of his arms.

"You do?" he asked, surprised.

"Yeah. You're the guy who's always in the library, reading."

"I don't read all the time."

She was amused. "What's the matter? Are you ashamed of being smart?"

"No." He paused. "How do you know I'm in the library a lot?"

She turned back to her mirror with cold cream and a clean cotton ball. "You mean, you never see me in the library? I'm in there a lot, too, I just keep out of sight." She wiped at her lipstick. "Who's your favorite author?"

He shrugged. "I have so many. I read a lot of sci-fi and fantasy. How about you?"

"James Joyce. Have you read *Ulysses?*"

"Tried. I'm not sure I understood it."

She nodded. "You're honest. Who really understands that book? I like Dante as well, his *Inferno.*"

"That's a hell of a literary work."

She stared at him in the mirror. "Hell interests me."

She might have been teasing, he wasn't sure. "Why?" he asked.

She shook her head. "No why. It's just what holds my attention." She stopped. "Do you think I'm weird?"

He was careful. "I hardly know you."

"What did you say your name was?"

"Mark Charm."

"What kind of name is that?"

He kept a straight face. "Mark is a common name, Jessa."

She laughed. "You have a sense of humor, I like that." She gestured. "I suppose I should cover myself, but you seem like the kind of guy who likes to look at half-naked girls."

He felt bold. "Actually, I like totally naked girls." He couldn't believe he had just said that to her, especially to her. She continued to smile.

"Did you really like my performance?" she asked.

"Yeah," he said seriously. "I loved it. When you're onstage, you are Ebo."

"What did you think of David Simmons?"

"He was OK."

"Just OK?"

"Yeah. He was no you."

She was pleased. "Between you and me, I think he sucks. I hate it when he kisses me. I always want to vomit in his face."

Mark was happy to hear that. "And I thought you two were an item."

She lost her smile. "Why? Because he follows me around campus? He just doesn't know how to take no for an answer."

Mark had a sudden crisis of confidence. Now was the perfect time to ask her out. They would not be alone forever. He was on a roll and she seemed to like him. But his brain froze up, he couldn't think of anything to say—not even a miserable comment on the unseasonably dry weather they were having. He noticed her studying him in her bright mirror.

"Is there something wrong?" she asked.

"No." He stood. "I should be going."

She was too cool to be offended. "All right. It was nice meeting you, Mark. Maybe some time we can talk again."

She was practically inviting him out!

Ask her out! Do it!

He nodded. "We'll see. Nice talking to you."

He was out the door before she could respond.

Outside, in the warm night air, he could have shot himself.

"We'll see?" he swore to himself. "Damn!"

Well, he thought, he couldn't go back inside and try again, not tonight at least. But it hadn't gone badly, he had to admit to himself. She had flirted with him and said how much she disliked David Simmons. That was more than he could have hoped for when the evening started. He would talk to her Monday at lunch, ask her out then.

Mark left the campus feeling high.

The feeling did not remain. His mother was ill; she had advanced bone cancer. The tumors had already spread to her brain, and now it was a waiting game. Even the recently engineered genetic miracle drugs could not stop the spread of the disease. The doctors said they could keep her comfortable, nothing more. But comfort was a relative term. She was only free from pain when she had a milligram of the designer Txex flowing through her veins. Otherwise, simply breathing was unbearable. He had been spending most every free minute with her because there were only the two of them. His father had died in a fire when he was ten and his mother had never remarried. He didn't know what he was going to do when she did finally die, didn't know if he could take it.

Perhaps his trying to ask Jessa out had been an act of desperation. Yet he didn't believe he was trying to replace the single person who had ever truly loved him with a fresh love. He believed his infatuation with Jessa was an entity unto itself. It didn't matter that his mother's name was Jessica—that was a coincidence. There were such things.

Mark drove his five-year-old used electric Saturn toward the hospital. There weren't many fossil fuel cars left in Los Angeles, but gasoline stations died slowly. He passed two on the way to the UCLA Medical Center. He had never driven an internal combustion engine car and hated the noise and smell. He didn't mind the gasoline, though, and he had his reasons. He could be a little wild at times, when he was feeling hyper or distraught.

He didn't know how to handle the pain his mother's agony brought him. When he was with her, he appeared to be composed. He would talk and rub her back and read to her. They'd watch TV or else play a computer game together. He tried to let her win, but her concentration was fading. The doctors said she would be one of the first people to die of cancer in L.A. that year. He didn't understand why they had shared that fact with him. It made him want to take the hospital and turn it to ash.

In his mind Mark could picture it burning as he turned off Wilshire Boulevard and saw it standing straight and tall. Many considered it the finest hospital in the land, but to him it was a witch's castle. Ebo's spells haunted its corridors. Even if

Jessa made love to him all night, it would not bring his mother back once she was gone. Nothing would—the universe did not allow library books to be returned and repaired once they were damaged and lost. Of course not, how could it? Universal logic dictated that hope pitted against logic was hopeless.

Still, he prayed for a miracle. Fool.

Her room was on the ninth floor. The nighttime view of Westwood and neighboring Beverly Hills was calming, but since it was past visiting hours, he knew he would have little chance to enjoy it. He would just have started to talk to her when a nurse would appear and kick him out. But they knew she was dying, and they always gave him a few minutes. The hospital staff weren't bad, he realized, they just couldn't heal her.

His mom was asleep when he entered the room. From the sound of her breathing, shallow and labored, he decided not to wake her. Better the dreams of the unconscious than the nightmares of the awake. He sat on a chair near her bed and stared at her wrinkled face. His mom was only forty-five but she looked seventy. His eyes burned as he watched her withered body struggle with the spreading disease, and his unshed tears washed away the remains of his talk with Jessa. He knew what would happen when his mother died—it was inevitable. He had only one mother and she had only one life. That was the basic insanity of life—it snuffed out so easily. He realized that all over the world people were suffering that very moment. But right then, staring at his mom, he felt he lived alone in an empty universe.

He didn't touch her because he didn't want to wake her.

He didn't want to wake himself, either, and kill his useless hope.

He left after five minutes. The nurses never knew he had been there.

The road home was lonely. He kept trying to think of Jessa, but his mother's face would rise up and blot it out. Her pain would burn through his wishes. The image of fire, more than of drowning, haunted him as he passed another gasoline station. Not really thinking what he was doing—but nevertheless knowing full well—he pulled his electric car into a station and popped the trunk.

Mark kept a five-gallon can in his trunk. He brought it with him because, well, he occasionally liked to fill it with fuel. And this fuel, well, he occasionally liked to burn it—and other things, too. But he didn't think of himself as a pyromaniac because he didn't feel the need to burn things every day. He didn't get off on the act, sexually, like most pyros did. He only burned things when everything inside him got so pent up that he felt he would explode. Or else fry. Yes, he only burned things when he was hot inside. It was really very simple, and he didn't think it was too weird. Of course, he usually tried not to think about it at all.

Mark purchased the gasoline—filled the can to the top—put it back in the trunk, and drove off. His direction was not aimless. He lived in Pacific Palisades—wedged between Malibu and Santa Monica—and was fond of hiking in the Malibu hills above the cool blue ocean and the big movie-star homes. The previous month he had stumbled upon a huge house about two months shy of completion. He had witnessed the rich white owner chewing out the hardworking Hispanic foreman, and Mark had thought the rich cat should not be so rude. Not that the idea of burning down the house had come to him then, but the seed had been planted. Yet in a way a part of him was always on the lookout for something to burn.

He probably was a pyromaniac.

He was a mystery even to himself. Yet for an enigma his desires were surprisingly simple when he was in the dark mood. He just loved to watch a fire, to feel the spark of reflected light on his pupils, to sense the hypnotic heat on his face, and taste the bitter smoke. Since he had been young he had loved and even worshipped fire.

Mark drove deep into Malibu and parked down the hill from the construction sight. Carrying the heavy can, he hiked up a dirt path leading off the long winding Malibu road. The property was plum, although there were as yet no trees to give it shade, only Malibu's infamous late autumn dry bushes, fuel for fires and nationwide headlines. The house, three stories of exquisite angles and lacquered wood, had both mountain and ocean views and was far off the beaten path. He had never burned down anything so expensive; previously it had been just a shed here, an outhouse there. He was excited but worried as well. The cops and firefighters would come quick.

The hike up to the place proved harder than he had imagined. But if the smell of fire pleased him, then the aroma of gasoline sparked his imagination. He was panting heavily when he crested the bluff that overlooked the house, the dark swath of the Pacific Ocean stretching endlessly off to his right, two miles distant. The house was Mediterranean—white stucco with an orange-tiled roof—and it had a dozen oval windows that faced the sea. In the faint light from the moon he could make out the beige wall-to-wall carpet through the rows of glass. The thought of the soon-to-be-exploding silicon was pleasant. He set the can down and contemplated his next move.

He realized that the place might already have an alarm system installed. The owner—paranoid bastard that he was—would have installed one the moment the walls were in place. For that reason Mark focused on the stunted power pole that had been erected in a corner of the property. He decided to take that out after he disabled the backup battery. He could clip the wires more effectively than burning them, even though he wanted to smell the rubbery smoke. That night, thinking of his screwed-up life and his poor mom, he wanted to burn the world.

Besides his big can of gasoline and box of matches, he had brought a pair of sharp pliers and a tiny pair of Nikon binoculars—precious items his trunk was never without. Huddling beside the power pole, he thought of the rudeness of the owner and how the guy deserved to have his dream house torched. No doubt, in those last minutes, Mark tried to rationalize his act. But the truth was he just wanted to watch the place burn, it would make one hell of an inferno up there on the hill.

He thought of hell and Jessa's literary reference as his pliers sliced through the wire and the black coil fell lifeless at his feet. Hell—a place to be feared, but a favorite fantasy destination of his. He had not read Dante's *Inferno,* but he would search for it in the library on Monday. Perhaps Dante had been a pyro, maybe Jessa was—she had obviously loved casting her alter ego's curses in the play. That was the trouble with obsessive people, Mark knew, they could learn to enjoy anything.

He wanted to enter the house carefully, but after crawling around the exterior he came away with a healthy respect for its solid wood doors. He ended up breaking a pane of glass in a door with a rock.

He tried to cushion the blow so the glass would fall inside, but the glass shards fell all around him. The impact and noise made him jump, although he doubted that anyone could have heard it. Nevertheless, he picked up his pace as he reached inside and twisted the dead bolt on the door free.

In a moment he was inside and restlessly tossing gasoline around, an ounce in the downstairs bathroom, generous amounts over the plush living room carpet, a steady trail up the mahogany stairs to the second and third floors. Because the night was warm, the fumes came quick and thick. For him it was an aroma to stimulate hunger. There was an instant when he even thought of splashing a little gasoline on himself and turning himself into a human torch.

But he knew that would hurt.

In the master bedroom, on the third floor, he dumped what was left on a stack of boxes. He didn't pause to see what they contained.

Then he did something foolish. Standing beside the boxes, the empty can at his feet, he reached for his lighter and playfully spun the wheel. Crazily he wanted to challenge the fire, his life against it. All along he had planned to light the fire when he was standing next to the front door. But now he wanted to ride the devil's roller coaster, see if he could outrun the orange tongues of flame down the gasoline-soaked stairs. The flame sprung to life in his right hand; he leaned over and touched it to the stack of mysterious boxes.

They began to burn, upward of course, but the fire also followed the gasoline along the floor as well. He stared at it with detached fascination—he could have been watching a movie. But when the bedroom carpet began to burn, he was shocked out of his stupor and realized the folly of his act. He was one second shy of cremating himself when he took off for the door and the stairs.

Halfway down the stairs the fire caught up to him. Yet it did not burn him, probably because he was moving too fast. It was as if he and the fire were in a dead heat, but it couldn't take the lead on him. When he hit the living room floor, however, things got spooky. The flames exploded in every direction, and for several seconds he found himself trapped in the middle of the room. Still, it was odd—it was as if the flames had decided to show him mercy and retreated several feet. They seemed to be studying him as he studied them and that was the first time he really understood fire as a living entity. It had sparks for neurotransmitters, orange flames for limbs, and heat for blood. He felt his own blood boil as the flames stared at him with the smoldering eyes of cremation. The fire would only study him so long, he knew.

He escaped from the house by diving headfirst out a window. He was lucky because he landed in a pile of sand and—except for a couple scratches on his face and arms—the glass did him no real damage. A perverted but powerful protector seemed to enfold him. The night was turning out to be a blast after all—he wanted to scream. Adrenaline was pumping as he grabbed his binoculars and pliers and ran full speed down the hill. It was amazing he didn't stumble because he kept looking back to watch the fire. The house was going up quickly; when the firefighters arrived they would have only ash to hose down. As the windows exploded, they sounded like human souls being consumed by demons. He laughed as he ran, so loud he could have been screaming.

His red Saturn—what other color would he have bought?—was where he had left it. He had forgotten to lock it; no matter, he was inside and barreling down the road within seconds. His goal was to reach the top of a hill that overlooked the house. But to reach it he first had to drive a mile down toward the ocean. The house was now off to his right and above him. Nothing more now than a box of oversize fireflies waging a version of World War Three. Paranoia began to dampen his enthusiasm because there was still a chance he would run into a cop while fleeing from the scene.

But he fretted unnecessarily. It wasn't until he was parked and sitting on the high hill, staring down at his handiwork, that the first police cruisers and fire trucks reached the road that led up to the house. He noted their leisurely pace; they knew the house was history. But he didn't underestimate the cops, they would be scanning the area for the fiend who had torched the place. Virtually all pyromaniacs were caught watching the fires that they themselves had started. Somehow, that didn't seem right to him.

But he would not be caught. He had chosen the perfect place to watch. He could get off the hill by taking any one of three dirt roads, two down to the sea, the other deeper into the Malibu hills. For now he was in heaven, sitting cross-legged all by himself on that hill, observing the flames through his small glass eyes. His mother and Jessa were momentarily forgotten. It was always that way right after he had had his fix.

The breeze blew up the hills; he could smell the smoke, taste it even. Not for a second did he lament the work his single act had wasted. It seemed a perfect end for the home. The place could have sat there for fifty years, housing any number of boring families. But this way it got to expend all its energy in a single glorious night. In some mysterious way, he knew he would do the same with his life.

Then Mark saw him. As the police and firefighters scattered around the house, Mark scanned the terrain with his binoculars and caught sight of a dark figure on top of a hill off to his left and farther back from the ocean. The person appeared to be male, tall, and dressed in a long black coat. From a ray of light from the fire Mark caught sight of the guy's binoculars—a stab of reflected orange on a hard lens—and realized that the guy was staring at him and not at the fire. The man's binoculars must have been stronger than his. The moment Mark focused on him, the guy turned away and walked into the hills.

A cold shiver of intuition swept over Mark, a shiver that was not warmed by the hot smoke blowing his way. The man was not running toward the police; he was not going to report him. But Mark knew he would see the man again.

2

The following Monday at school Mark was sitting alone outside on a wooden bench, eating the lunch he had packed the previous night. He had a turkey sandwich, potato chips, and a can of Coke. The Coke was warm but he didn't care because he was hungry and it helped to wash down the food. Since his mother had gone in the hospital, he had been living mostly on sandwiches, which was fine with him. He liked fast-food hamburgers, also good because he didn't exactly have a huge food budget. Even though he and his mom lived in rich Pacific Palisades, their rented home had to be the smallest in the city. He couldn't turn around in the bathroom without bumping into the recessed toilet paper holder. He worked at a record store after school to supplement their meager income. Before she had gotten sick, his mom had helped run a day-care center, no big bucks there. The past Saturday he had bought a large turkey and cooked it himself. He planned to live off it for the rest of the week, along with a bag of potatoes. He wasn't fussy when it came to food.

Jessa, out of nowhere, sauntered up to him. Against every rule in the book, she was smoking a cigarette and drinking a beer. Her hair was pulled back and she wore not a spot of makeup. Her blue jean cutoffs were short and tight, but her yellow shirt was loose and long. Her brown sandals flopped, but her walk was still smooth because of the way she carried herself. She smiled when she saw him; her teeth were not perfect but her lips were—that was all that mattered.

"Hey, Mark," she said. "What the hell are you doing?"

He held up his sandwich. "Eating. Want a bite?"

She surprised him by accepting. In fact, she took his sandwich and didn't give it back. Maybe she liked turkey, he thought, or maybe it was him. She chewed loudly and took a swig of beer.

"This is good," she said.

"Hungry?" he asked.

"Starved."

"Finish it then."

She shook her head and forced the sandwich back on him. "No, you're a growing boy. You need your nourishment." She had more beer and gestured to the bench. "Why are you eating here? Only losers eat here."

He had to chuckle. He was happy to see her again.

"Maybe I am a loser," he said. "Maybe it's a contagious condition."

She liked that. "Not you. You know, you had a lot of nerve coming into my dressing room last Friday night. I was practically naked."

He nodded. Her approaching him gave him unexpected confidence. "Practically. What did you do this weekend?"

She rolled her eyes and plopped down beside him. "Got wasted. Painted, worked on my book."

"You're writing a book?"

She studied him and then frowned. "I haven't told anyone except you. Why did I do that? You better not talk about it to anyone." Her tone was intense.

"Don't worry, I have a short memory. What's it about?"

She contemplated her almost empty beer can before throwing it in the garbage. She concentrated on her cigarette. He hadn't known she smoked; he knew almost nothing about her. Except that she was even more inviting close up than from afar. Her sober gray eyes were flecked with a cat's green— twilight mingled with myth. She chewed gum as she smoked. Her pale skin appeared too soft for her personality, and he wondered what it would be like to hold her in his arms and give her mouth to mouth.

"It's a complicated story," she said finally. "It starts fast and then takes off. But I don't know where it will end." She paused and took a drag on her cigarette. "I don't even know if it should end."

"What genre is it?" he asked.

"Sci-fi. Horror. It's a love story." She flashed him a wicked grin. "It's brilliant—it can't be classified."

He was interested. "I'd like to read it when you're done with it."

She threw her cigarette down and stepped on it. Her gaze shifted, suddenly far off. "No. I told you, it won't end. I'll just keep writing it and that's the way it will be."

She was trying to tell him something, he realized, more than the obvious. But he didn't understand her moods and therefore moved cautiously.

"I'm sure it's a wonderful story," he said gently.

She stared at him. "I bet you're wondering why I'm sitting here talking to you."

The thought had crossed his mind. He shrugged. "You're bored?"

A shy smile. "I've been thinking about you, Mark. I haven't been able to stop thinking about you. But before you let my remarks go to your head, I have to add that you're not that great looking."

He wished she hadn't added that last sentence. It

made his comeback difficult. He gulped and muttered, "I have other redeeming qualities."

She touched his arm and nodded sympathetically. "That's why I've been thinking of you." She paused. "What do you think of me?"

He couldn't look at her. "You seem like a nice girl."

She laughed. "God! I hope not! Is that how you see me? I'm far from nice. I am corrupt to the bone and assumed that's why you sought me out."

He glanced over. "Honestly, Jessa, I don't know anything about you. Just that you're a great actress."

She came closer and spoke confidentially. "And that I'm kind of sexy?"

He relaxed a notch. "Yeah, I'd say so."

She sat back, satisfied. "You want to cut class this afternoon?"

He had an important test in chemistry. But Jessa was biochemistry and anatomy and physiology—she won hands down.

"Where do you want to go?" he asked. He couldn't believe she was asking him out and chose not to reflect on what it meant for his future. But he was sure, that night, he would think of nothing else. Assuming of course that they had fun together.

She considered. "To the beach. You have a car?"

"Yeah." He had to work after school as well. He'd probably get fired for not showing up, but perhaps he could call from the road. He added, "I like the beach."

"Cool." She stood. "I want to get a few things out of my car. Do you have trunks?"

He stood. "I have tennis shorts in my locker. They'll have to do."

She nodded. "I have a suit in my locker. I swim in the school pool early every morning." She reached for another cigarette and cleared her throat. "It clears all the crap out of my lungs. How about I meet you at your car in fifteen minutes?"

He was humming. "Great. It's a red Saturn, in the south corner."

She lit her cigarette and caught him staring at the flame on her lighter. She didn't wink at him, but she came close. It made him wonder.

"I know, Mark," she said.

They went to Zuma Beach, at the north end of Malibu. The waves were breaking fierce and close to the shore—a dangerous combination. It was early November but hot as mid-July. The chalk sign on the lifeguard station put the water temperature at 65°F—not bad for California's coast. Mark had hardly stretched out their towels when Jessa wanted to go in the water. Her bathing suit was a single piece, navy blue, tight on the butt. She was more muscular undressed—it must have been her regular swimming. She still had a cigarette in her mouth. Sitting on a towel, he took off his pants reluctantly. He had skinny legs.

"You can swim, can't you?" she asked.

He nodded as he undressed. "I surf, so I know what it's like to be pounded. We better get past the waves as quickly as possible."

Jessa regarded the ocean. "Nonsense. I want to body surf."

He stood and pulled off his shirt. "Great way to break your neck. I have an old friend who was made a quadriplegic at this beach."

The comment stopped her. "He is a head on a pillow?"

"Yeah. He can't even feed himself."

The image sobered her. "It's hard to imagine living like that."

"He's a brave guy. Never complains."

Jessa considered a moment, her gaze focused far away, as it had been when he asked about her book. Then she shook her head and took his hand and smiled. She pulled him toward the water. Her cigarette fell in the sand.

"I like to dive in," she said. "I like to feel my heart stop."

"Sounds like fun," Mark said without enthusiasm.

She did indeed dive in, before him, and screamed as the first big wave crashed on the back of her head. Seconds later she resurfaced, laughing.

As the next wave approached, she swam furiously. He called out for her to be careful—six-foot waves were breaking in three feet of water. Even standing in the shallow water of the Pacific, he could feel the power of the rip tide. Of course she ignored him, she was a nut, he knew that about her already. The thick wave caught her and flipped her over and jackknifed her down into the white wash. But, once again, she resurfaced and howled at him about how much fun it was.

"Come on!" she yelled.

He couldn't appear a coward, not and hope to sleep with her. He dived in and swam toward her, the cold biting his skin. They both rolled in the strength of the current. Within minutes they were over a hundred yards down the beach from their towels, a fresh set of waves looming on the horizon. She told him that he had to ride a wave with her.

"I want to see what you're made of," she said.

"You have to be careful to pull out at the last second," he warned. "You really can get hurt."

She shook her head. "Trust me, it's impossible for us to get hurt."

He wasn't sure what that meant. Had God given her a guarantee? Mark wasn't sure if he believed in God anymore, after seeing his mother suffer the way she had, but he wanted, at least, to believe in love. Looking at Jessa's face drenched in salt water, her dark hair plastered to her skull above her wide eyes, he wanted to trust that the universe would give him a chance, if not a guarantee. A huge wave was coming, he could not die on this happy day. He turned and swam hard beside her, brushing her side with his left hand. She squealed with delight.

"This is so cool!" she said.

The wave lifted them up and shoved them forward. The worst thing happened immediately—what Mark had feared the most—his legs began to be lifted over his head. He was about to be flipped. Immediately he thrust out his arms, and not a second too soon. The wave threw him down into the shallow surf and his palms and wrists slapped the sand bottom—it could have been a stone wall. The shock reverberated throughout his body. Yet he had spared his head and neck. The surf continued to shove him toward the shore, and when he was finally able to surface, he was in one foot of water. Jessa lay in the white wash beside him, panting with pleasure.

"Did you almost die?" she asked, excited.

He rubbed his aching wrists. They were both sprained, he was sure, he wouldn't be able to move them tomorrow. "Yeah," he muttered.

She stood and he caught a glimpse of her right breast. The wave had done a number on her suit. She covered herself back up, slowly.

"Want to do it again?" she asked.

He got up with effort. The roll in the sand had scraped his legs as well. Blood dripped from his knees. That was one nasty ride. He did have a crush on her and didn't want to look chicken, but she was going to get him killed. He shook his head.

"I think I'll go work on my tan," he said.

Her expression mocked him. "I told you, you can't get hurt."

He flexed his wrists. "I believe you."

She grabbed his hand. "OK. I'll lie on the beach with you, as long as you massage me all over with suntan lotion."

She didn't have to twist his arm. "All over?" he asked.

Her eyes shone mischievously. "As much as you can handle."

A half hour later under a brilliant sky he was still rubbing her back, under her suit, getting close to her butt but not having the nerve to go there. For her part Jessa could have been asleep. Her breathing was deep and regular. His wrists were killing him, but he could not have been more satisfied. Yet he wondered how his mother was doing. It was after three—he hadn't called her yet today as he usually did.

"How are you feeling?" she asked, her face turned away from him pressed against the towel.

"Good."

"You are troubled."

"Oh? Are you a mind reader?"

She turned her head in his direction but didn't open her eyes. "Yes. That is exactly what I am. Is it your mother?"

He was astounded. "How do you know about my mother?"

"People at school told me she was sick."

"Which people?" He didn't have that many friends.

"People. They said she was close to dying. Is that true?"

Mark had to concentrate to keep rubbing her. "Yeah. She has cancer throughout her body. The drugs aren't working."

"I'm sorry," she said with feeling.

"It's not your fault."

She raised her head and looked at him. "How do you know it's not my fault?"

He stopped. "I don't understand what you mean."

She turned away. "You go to see her every night, feeling helpless. You would do anything in the world to make her all right but you can't."

He had a lump in his throat. Although he didn't want to show grief in front of her, certainly not tears, it was hard to remain calm. It *was* as if she could read his mind.

"It's not easy to watch her suffer," he said.

She sat up and took his hands in hers. "Do you want to get past that?"

"How?"

Her gaze was intense. "Have you heard of MAZE?"

The name was familiar, but he couldn't pinpoint

exactly what he knew and where he had read about it. The break in his memory was disturbing because he felt he had studied the subject at some length. Recently, too. There must have been an article in the paper, but the details were inches beyond his reach. The frustration and certainty were reminiscent of déjà vu. Jessa nodded to herself as he fought with his brain.

"Its technical name is methlenedioxy amphetamine z-emertrine," she explained. "It's a cousin of LSD, but they're not close cousins."

Mark nodded. It came back to him now, parts, but the long name she quoted didn't ring a bell. He was no fool when it came to designer drugs, which had been the craze since the turn of the century. Not that he was into drugs; he didn't like to have his reality altered. It brought him no relief; it just made a greater enemy of time. One always had to come down.

"I've read about it." He paused. "You have some?"

"Yes." She moved closer, sitting between his legs. "It's hard to get, but I have friends in the right places."

"And money," he interrupted. He had heard the gossip—Jessa lived in a huge home overlooking the ocean. Her parents were Hollywood producers with two sitcoms in syndication. He knew the shows—they were awful. She accepted his correction.

"Lots of money," she said. "They make it down in Mexico. They have a whole clinic devoted to its use. It's perfectly legal down there."

"You mean it's tolerated. The Mexican government does not approve of MAZE."

"You're wrong. If they didn't approve of it, the clinic would not exist. It's not a normal drug. It opens you up, lets you see what is real. It's not addictive."

Mark had read that for many it was psychologically addictive—in the extreme.

"You mean physically," he said.

Jessa shook her head. "You have to be open here. MAZE is a great discovery. It may change the face of humanity, when the fear surrounding it disappears. Science is moving deeper into space; DNA has been mapped; disease is almost to be wiped out. These are exciting times to be alive. But scientific discoveries pale when it comes to the exploration of the mind. MAZE is an important key to that exploration."

He was disappointed because he found her argument naive. "If it is such an exciting time to be alive," he asked, "why do you need to take drugs to enhance your excitement?"

She was not rebuffed. "Let me answer your question with another question. How can you judge something you know nothing about?"

"It's a psychoactive drug. What else do I need to know?"

She gripped his hands. "It's much more than that. MAZE allows you to see what cannot be seen. It leads you into secret realms that have never before been explored. It's not a simple hallucinogenic. When I'm on MAZE, I see and understand more than when I'm straight."

"Are you on it now?" he asked.

She paused. "No."

"Are you sure?"

"I'm sure." She reached for her bag. "But I have two doses with me. It works best when smoked. We can do it here if you want, or else go to my house. No one is home."

He stopped her. "This won't help me with my mother."

She froze, her head down, and when she spoke it was with more gentleness than he had heard from her before. "I didn't mean to imply your mother's pain could be removed by getting high with me. I'm sorry, Mark."

He let go of her and sat back. "Why is it important to you that we do this together? Personally, I'd prefer to get to know you with my brain cells functioning normally."

She opened her purse and removed two tiny plastic bags. She held them up for him to see. The crystalline powder was white and—if he remembered right—tasteless. It glistened in the sunlight; angel's poison. But she was right—it didn't work if it passed through the digestive tract. He was suddenly remembering all kinds of things about it.

Yet there was one thing about MAZE he couldn't recall.

Something crucial. His mind refused to focus on it.

"It takes a long time to get to know another person," she explained. "Who knows what can happen between now and tomorrow? I want to take it with you so we can get to know each other quickly."

"You certainly don't have much faith in our long-term prospects."

"Do you?"

He shrugged. "I like you so far."

She was intent. "But my interest in drugs upsets you, admit it."

He hesitated. "Yes."

"And there is nothing you do, privately, that you wouldn't be ashamed to let me know about?"

Once again, he felt as if she could see through him. For the first time he wondered if the drug bestowed psychic powers. Her gray eyes were so bright, he suspected they must glow in the dark. Maybe she was a witch and wanted to get him stoned so she could sacrifice him on a black altar set up in her basement. He supposed there were worse ways to go. The way the crystals sparkled in the sunlight, plus those eyes, stimulated his curiosity. Still, it was one thing to burn down a house to release stress, but he didn't want to fry his nervous system.

"I didn't say that," he replied.

"Tell me what it is."

"What what is?"

"Your big secret. I know you have one. You can tell me, I won't tell anyone."

He was embarrassed. "With me, what you see is what you get."

She snorted. "Liar. I used to watch you even before you barged in on me last Friday. You have too much on your mind for a simpleton. Your mother is not your only source of grief. Tell me what it is."

"No."

"Why not?" she demanded.

"I hardly know you." He stared at the drugs in her hands. "You just want me to take that so you can screw with my brain."

"It's not the only thing I want to screw with, Mark." She flashed him a sly smile and shook the Baggies. "Come on, once won't kill you."

He didn't know why he agreed.

3

They passed the house he had burned down on the way to his place. They had decided his house—empty of parents for the foreseeable future—was a better location to take the MAZE. Catching sight of the blackened ruins up on the hill, Mark couldn't help but let his gaze linger and was fortunate he didn't drive off the road. Jessa didn't appear to notice the object of his distraction as she lit another cigarette. She looked good in her wet bathing suit, the wind in her hair.

"I love this road," Jessa said, referring to Pacific Coast Highway. "It's always crowded, always getting ripped up from mud slides, fires, earthquakes. The ocean is just waiting to wash over it, and my parents' house lies just off it." She glanced at him. "I guess you could call me a natural-disaster kind of girl."

"Do you have any brothers or sisters?"

"No. Do I need a sister? Aren't I enough for you?"

He smiled. "How long does the effect of the drug last?"

"Six hours."

"What should I expect?"

"Drop your expectations. That's when the interesting stuff happens."

"Tell me something about it. It will put my mind at ease."

She blew smoke. "You'll see reality. Be prepared."

Fortunately his house was clean. He only tidied up once a week, and he had done it over the weekend. Jessa headed straight for the shower. She left the door open but didn't invite him to join her. He might have peeked in but didn't want to appear to be a pervert. She showered and reappeared in ten minutes, her hair wrapped in a towel.

"Do you have a blow-dryer?" she asked.

"No."

"Does your mother?"

"It's at the hospital."

An awkward moment. "Sorry," she said.

He stepped toward the shower. "It's OK. It's what it is. Nothing's going to change it."

Jessa did not respond.

Twenty minutes later they were ready to take the drug. They sat on the couch in the living room.

Mark was hungry and wanted to eat first: turkey and potatoes. But Jessa stopped him, she said food tasted much better on MAZE.

"I thought you said the stuff made you throw up," he said.

"It does, at first. But after you vomit your guts out and the drug comes on, you'll be starving. Food on MAZE tastes incredible."

"I don't know if I like this. Why should I take anything that will make me throw up?"

"Because I want you to," she said simply.

"And if you want me to jump off a building?"

"You will do that as well." She leaned over and kissed his cheek. Her lips were warm and wet, nice. "Do you have a lighter?"

He didn't smoke but happened to have one in his pocket, big surprise. He took it out while she carefully poured the drug into a miniature pipe she had taken from her bag. Taking his lighter, she held the flame near the white crystals.

"The smoke enters cool and stimulating," she said. "You'll like it."

"Please don't vomit on me, when the time comes."

She held the pipe to her lips. "That won't be for twenty minutes. The nausea will pass swiftly. Then you will see."

"What you see? How often do you do this stuff?"

She teased the flame to the drug. "Only when I'm awake."

39

Jessa took a long drag on the burning crystals and held the smoke inside. The crystals went out immediately. She handed him the pipe and nodded for him to begin. Although he didn't smoke, being a pyromaniac, he was familiar with the sensation of smoke in his lungs. He lit the drug and sucked it in—the smoke was not irritating, and he was able to hold his breath a long time. Jessa was an expert—she didn't exhale until after he had. She took the pipe back.

"Now that wasn't bad," she remarked.

"I don't feel anything."

She teased. "Not even horny?"

"Did you offer to sleep with me just to get me to get high with you?"

"Maybe."

"That's what I thought," he muttered.

They smoked the remainder of the drug. Mark was surprised when he continued to feel nothing. Most drugs that were inhaled passed directly into the bloodstream and worked immediately. After all the MAZE was percolating in their veins, they continued to sit on the couch and look at each other.

"Maybe it will be you who throws up on me," she said.

"It will serve you right for twisting my arm."

"Don't be a stiff. Admit it, you wanted to try it the moment I brought it up. Besides, do you know how much we just smoked costs?"

"I can imagine. Where do you get the money?"

"Do I deal? Is that what you're asking?"

"No. But now that you mention it."

She was insulted. "I'm not a pusher. I have an inheritance. I use it as I please."

"Must be nice."

"Do you think I'm a snob?" she asked.

He chuckled. "I don't have to decide that now. According to you, in an hour or so I'll know everything about you."

"You may see some things that will shock you."

"Will I discover that you're an alien creature?"

She was grave. "Maybe worse. You have to stay cool."

"I'm cool," he assured her.

Twenty minutes later, as measured by the clock, he felt a wave of nausea sweep through his guts. He barely made it to the bathroom and was just leaving when Jessa barreled past him and slammed the door. The tiny house was not an ideal MAZE clinic, after all—it had only one restroom. He could hear Jessa retching on the other side of the door and not for the first time he wondered what the hell he had gotten himself into.

He returned to the living room and turned on the TV. Ten or fifteen minutes went by, and Jessa went from the bathroom to the kitchen. He heard her searching the cabinets for food, good luck. There was a horror film on Channel 1112—gray aliens taking over the world in catsup bottles. At least that was how the plot appeared to him. But when he thought about it he knew that couldn't be right. Then he realized he was watching a one-minute commercial. Odd, a moment ago it had seemed a lengthy feature. There was no movie, there were no aliens.

Yet he couldn't help feeling that *something* was near.

It was not mere paranoia. More like revelation.

The drug had kicked in early. He was high.

"Jessa," he called softly.

She came out of the kitchen with a turkey leg in her hand. When she smiled at him, the feeling of an observing presence retreated. No, it was as if her inner being merged with the presence and became less threatening. He began to feel as if the watching presence was not distinct from his mind at all. Perhaps it was his mind, a higher aspect of his consciousness. Perhaps all was one mind.

"You're tripping?" she asked.

He considered his answer for ages. "Yes."

"How do you feel?"

Another gap, longer than before. "I have no feelings."

She moved closer. He watched her chew, watched her saliva enter the meat in her mouth to begin the complex process of digestion. Her eating was the most primal of acts because all beings must eat to exist. He understood that bodies were nothing but digested food. She was pretty, Jessa Welling, but he could see the meat in her muscles, the fruits and the vegetables in her skin, the grains in her bones. A portion of everything she had ever assimilated in her life flowed through her veins as red corpuscles. The oxygen in her lungs was digested air.

She sat on the couch beside him, and he slowly reached out to touch her hair. His hand reached its goal only after a vast journey. Her hair was dead cells, rooted deep within her scalp. Such delicate hair attached to a hard skull. It was as if he sensed both her birth and death in that moment, and time did not merely stretch, it lost meaning altogether.

He knew then that she would not have a long life.

"Do you like it?" she asked.

"There's nothing to like."

She nodded. "You sense the abyss. It's all around us."

He reflected deeply. "We are not alone in the abyss."

He had her attention. "What else is there?"

"Someone."

"Who?"

He looked at her. "You."

She set her turkey leg down. "Who else?"

He looked deeper at her. "There is just you."

She appeared guarded. "Does that disturb you?"

"No. I know it is the way it is."

"Where are you?"

"Here," he said. "With you."

43

She blinked. "The drug has come on. I am with you."

But he shook his head. "There is more to this—there is a mystery here."

She took his hand. Digested food enclosed digested food. If he was starving, he knew, he could eat her and his body would survive on her flesh and blood. She was food; he was food. But they were sentient as well, aware that they were aware. That fact transcended their food bodies. But where did it lead? That was the mystery.

He understood that the MAZE had only begun.

Why were the aliens back on the TV?

They peeked at him from the tube, from the abyss.

MAZE had another meaning, she knew it and had lied to him.

"What is it?" she asked.

He stared. "You know. You can say."

She shook her head. "Keep looking, inside. What do you know?"

His hand remained in her hair. "That you test me. That you want something from me."

She nodded. "I do want something, and I need something. Tell me what it is."

"No. You test. You lie. You know."

"But what do I know?" she asked.

He gestured to their surroundings. "That nothing is as it appears."

She was intent. "True. What else?"

44

"You know. Your question is not sincere. Therefore, my answer will also have to be a lie. There is no point in your question."

She remained adamant. Her fingers gripped his.

"You know me," she said. "What do I want?"

"Love." The word came to him from far off.

"Why?"

"To survive. You need love."

Her face shone with lost love. Her tears glistened like MAZE crystals burning in the naked sun. There was no difference, he realized, between her pain and the drug. That was a deeper aspect of the mystery. Why she appeared to be all around him even as she sat before him. The abyss was filled with her pain.

The aliens on the TV clamored for his attention. They were beautiful but hideous as well, with transparent skulls. He could see their pink brains on the TV screen throb with pulsing blood. They were heads on a pillow. They had come to Earth in catsup bottles and taken over the planet. They had come in a moment, between the cracks of time, during a commercial break. They were not evil, they were merely older in the galactic scheme of things. They knew how to construct bizarre microscopes and peer into human brains. How to dissect human experience and keep what was good and discard what was bad.

There was not one mystery here but two.

One was deeper than the other.

He didn't know which was which. The aliens and the presence. But Jessa knew.

"That is true," she replied. "What else do I want from you?"

He understood that she was acknowledging her need for his love. She attempted to answer his question by directing him, or else misdirecting him. She was tied up with the mystery, as were the aliens with the transparent skulls. But the more they spoke to him from the TV, the more he understood that they were not visitors to Earth— they were the original inhabitants of the planet. They were normal people. They went to school, got jobs, married, and had children. Only they could not die, for some strange reason. Perhaps because their skulls were on view.

A wave of realization swept over him.

Layer upon layer, the pieces were beginning to fit.

It was the creatures who had put them in the TV that were the aliens. It was they who had sawed open the experience of humanity. They had shone a black light on their pink brains. They had covered the sun and blotted out the stars. They were the enemy, they were the old ones, but still they were not evil.

Was Jessa evil? She lied.

A mystery within a mystery.

"You want my power," he replied.

"What is your power?" she asked.

"You know. You lie."

"Tell me what it is. I don't know."

"No." He considered. "We are drugged."

"Yes." She was so close.

"What I say makes no sense."

"No," she said.

"The MAZE makes me see them. There are no aliens."

"Are you sure?"

He stared at her. He wanted to kiss her.

"Are you an alien?" he asked.

"No." She spoke the truth.

He was lost. "Who then? Who speaks?" He watched the TV. The people with the exposed brains were being herded into a warm blue bath. Their bodies fell away from their brains. In the blue bath they would float forever. They would never understand the mystery, that it even existed. But he understood, even if he did not know its solution. Yet it had something to do with his special power.

"You cannot have my power," he said. "It is not for you."

She was devastated. "I only want love."

Her remark teetered between revelation and deception. He understood the narrow gap between the two—especially in her presence. To touch her hair was the ultimate beguilment. He leaned close to kiss her, could smell the turkey on her breath. It was the same flesh he had eaten earlier in the day. They were one on the cellular level. She closed her eyes and waited for his lips. But as she did so a dark light went off in her brain, he saw it with his own eyes. Her skull became transparent, her brain tissue jiggled with her movements. But he could not dissect her thoughts, the mystery ran too deep. He drew back and wondered if he should kiss her at all. Her need for his love was at the core of this existence. Yet she continued to lie to him. She opened her eyes and stared at him with sorrow.

"What is wrong?" she asked.

"It's over." He didn't know why he had said that. Their relationship had just begun. Yet in a sense, he knew, it was ancient as well. It had existed before the aliens had come to Earth and floated their brains in the warm blue bath. She knew about the aliens and they knew about her. He wanted to kiss her, but to do so they would have to return to a previous age. She wanted that, he did not want it.

That was a large portion of the twin mysteries.

That was the danger. Her lies.

She wept. Her tears made no noise. She came close and kissed him, but he did not kiss her back. She whispered in his ear.

"We can go back, Mark," she said. "For a time it can be as it was before. You can love me again and I will love you as always. I will read my book to you. I will tell you my story. Lie naked beside me, sleep beside me, and I will tell you my secret tale. It is what you want, don't tell me it isn't, or you would not be here with me now."

48

He drew back. "What does MAZE mean? Is it a drug?"

"No," she said, her eyes dark. "It is a door."

He nodded. "That is true." He saw the TV. "And the aliens?"

She stood and offered her hand. "They are already here."

He took her hand and stood. The volume on the TV decreased. Outside the sun was eclipsed by a vast vessel in deep space. Shadows crossed the land and children were afraid. Dark brains floated in even darker blue fluid. He saw that both their brains had already been dissected. The aliens dimmed the interior and the exterior lights and cataloged the day's experiences on the memory chips of a computer network so vast that it stretched to the bowels of a steel world. They did so every day at this time, he knew.

Jessa was not one of them.

She said she was not and he believed her.

"Will you make love to me?" she asked.

"Yes," he whispered. "If you tell me your story."

"I will," she promised.

4

When he awoke it was dark and he was alone. He glanced at the clock—twelve o'clock, the witching hour. Where had Ebo, Jessa, gone? When he had lain down, she had snuggled naked beside him and pulled off his clothes. They might have had sex, he wasn't sure. He remembered moments of intense physical pleasure followed by those of falling into mysterious wells of black ink. She had recited a story to him, which he could not recall. Maybe it had only been in his head.

But in the soft yellow light of his desk lamp, he saw two strands of her dark hair on his pillow. He had slept with Jessa Welling, he thought in wonder, the girl of his dreams, but it had not been a dream. She must like him.

But where had she gone?

Mark heard a moan through the wall. He sat up

with a start. His mother's room was on the other side of the wall. Before she had gone into the hospital, she often awakened in the night in pain. He suspected he had imagined the sound because he had not called her once today. Guilt plagued his conscience. He got up and checked the house, just to satisfy himself that he was alone. Sure that he was, he returned to his room to dress. He was hopeful the MAZE had worn off but was not a hundred percent positive.

His experience on the drug was a blur. He knew there had been a recurring theme of aliens and Jessa's lies—typical hallucinogenic BS. Yet the intensity of the impressions had staggered him. While he had been under the drug's influence, he had been convinced he was seeing a greater reality. He chuckled to himself at the absurdity of it all. Where were the aliens and Jessa's lies now? Of course, she might have lied to him about the length of the drug trip. He still felt strangely altered. He didn't want to be high while driving to the hospital. He had to check on his mother, that was the priority.

Yet before he left he wanted to call Jessa, make sure she was OK. But he didn't know her number. He had never properly asked her out. Nothing about their relationship was normal, he realized. Three days ago he had been terrified to speak to her, and now they were getting high and having sex—or so he assumed. So many things had changed since last Friday, he wondered how it was all possible.

Mark dressed and left the house. He drove to the hospital at a leisurely clip. His senses were definitely still distorted: colors were brighter, shadows sharper, and time moved more slowly. The effect was not excessive and it didn't trouble him; he assumed it would all be gone by morning. He understood the trap Jessa had fallen into and he worried for her. MAZE was enticing; he had felt mysteriously powerful on the drug, as if he could know something just by putting his attention to it. But the drug had not taken away the wonder of the universe. To the contrary. With his expanded mental abilities he had felt many cosmic riddles present themselves to him. Most had been silly, of course, but he did understand why Jessa found the altered reality difficult to give up.

There was no question in his mind that she was addicted to the drug. Although he was curious to try it again, he knew he would not. He cared for her but didn't want to become her.

He wished he could remember if they had had sex.

As Mark entered the hospital a cold foreboding swept over him. He had not called his mom, it was true, but she had not called him, either. There had been no messages on his machine, which he now found odd. He hoped she was not feeling sicker.

Cold foreboding turned to icy horror when he

entered her room. Her bed was empty, there would have been no reason to move her. He ran to the nurses' station. An RN with a face as wide as a pillow and skin the color of spoiled buttermilk sat alone at the desk. She was reading a paperback novel—sex and mystery in paradise. She glanced up with a bored expression.

"May I help you?" she asked.

"Where is Jessica Charm? She was in Room Nine Sixty-two."

The nurse spoke matter-of-factly. "She died this evening. Her body's down in the morgue."

Mark took a moment. "No."

The nurse consulted a chart. "She died at six thirty-five. Are you family?"

He felt so small, so insignificant. As if his life were of no consequence because his mother's life was of no consequence in this sterile building. The nurse showed not a trace of compassion, obviously anxious to get back to her book. It was a quiet evening and Mark was clearly messing it up. He backed off a step and felt himself sink two feet into the floor. He was no longer under the influence of the drug. He was falling through the scenery of an empty universe. He wanted to shout at the nurse and tell her how dear his mother had been. But all that came out was a feeble remark.

"I was her only family," he said.

Mark turned and left the hospital. He didn't remember climbing into his car, but minutes later he was racing along the freeway, lights and signs flashing by like posts set in place by a lunatic with bad eyesight. Guilt burned a hole in his heart, loss filled it with more guilt. The one night he had not come to see his mother, she had died. Died alone, without her only son to bid her farewell. He had been too busy tripping, too absorbed in a girl he hardly knew to hold his mother's hand as she left the earth. Now he would never hold her hand again. She was down in the morgue, the nurse said. He was down there as well. He wasn't dead, but he didn't want to live—there was little difference.

He drove to the far side of L.A. before he realized he wouldn't be able to escape his grief. Yet he couldn't bear it, and it was not merely a question of not having enough strength. His mother had been the center of his universe for so long it was as if the universe could not exist without her in it. He could not breathe and felt he had no right to walk around like a normal person. Still, he had to live because he could not simply order his body to die. Desperate, he reached for the one thing he knew could help him.

He needed to burn.

He needed to burn a great deal.

Mark drove toward an oil refinery located at the edge of San Bernardino Valley, close to the desert. By no coincidence he knew where all the refineries were in southern California. This refinery in particular had attracted his attention because it was small and almost devoid of security. Of course, it wasn't as if he had planned to steal a gasoline truck to start the mother of all fires. Yet he had worked out—in remarkable detail—the ingredients that would be necessary to create such an inferno.

The conditions that night met his three main criteria: the weather had to be hot and dry, and the Santa Ana winds had to be blowing. Those wicked desert winds, that sucked the moisture from the skin as easily as from the withering autumn plants. Mark knew if he so much as lit a match in the right part of town he could send every firefighter in the state running for his hose. But with a thousand gallons of gasoline, he believed he could start a fire that could not be stopped.

But why? Why do it?

Simply because he had to. He felt it.

The odd thing was, it didn't seem to be *his* feeling.

Even to relieve him, this sounded like too much.

The aliens on the TV were talking again.

Mark kept driving toward the refinery.

It was a mom-and-pop shop. Only five trucks that made deliveries to small local industries. Yet the company didn't merely store fuel—it had a row of pumps scattered out back in a field so drenched with oil that a dinosaur might have recognized a decomposed ancestor. The refinery equipment must have been built back in the sixties by an acid-popping engineer who had been five decades ahead of the designer drug craze. It was such a mess of creaking and twisted machinery that Mark didn't understand how it could have produced a pint of gasoline to pass government inspection. He had once thought of burning the place down, just for kicks. Fortunately he hadn't, for tonight one of their trucks would serve a much greater purpose.

As he had expected, there was no guard in sight. Mark parked three blocks away, behind a deserted warehouse, and walked back to the refinery. He moved swiftly. It was two in the morning, and he had the block to himself. The twenty-foot fence that surrounded the refinery was a joke. He was over it in less than a minute. The gasoline trucks were parked behind a squat gray office building. He figured he would have to break into the building to get the keys to a truck. How pleased he was to discover the keys in the ignition of the last truck he examined. It was a small matter to break the driver's side window.

He ran into a problem then, however. The gasoline-powered truck's tank was empty, and Mark thought that he was going to have to start the facility's main pumps to refill it. But studying the various hoses on the truck, he figured he'd be better off draining the gasoline from another truck. He couldn't easily hot wire these vehicles as they were relatively new and therefore difficult to steal.

The entire procedure took Mark over an hour, longer than he wanted. Breaking the window on the truck disturbed him, which was odd, because obviously he didn't mind causing destruction by fire. Somehow whatever the fire took was OK. He knew it was illogical, but that was how he felt.

Mark headed back to Pacific Palisades with the truck. The hot wind was at his back, and he saw fire on the horizon. His mother was lying on a cold slab in a hospital basement—perhaps he would warm her up soon. It was conceivable that the fire he planned to start would sweep over west L.A. He hoped so, he didn't feel like going to school tomorrow.

Mark lived in Pacific Palisades, but his house was far from the most exclusive neighborhood of that city, known as the Highlands. The area was a city unto itself. Set two miles back from Sunset Boulevard in a lovely valley reminiscent of Napa Valley in northern California, it boasted many of the finest homes in the L.A. area. Hollywood's bigwigs, along with some rock stars and other hip millionaires, lived there. Mark knew the valley well; he had often hiked on the dusty trails that wound through the hills that enclosed the valley. This time of year the valley was as combustible as a thatched hut.

Once again, he wouldn't need a truckload of fuel to start a devastating fire, but his goal was greater than that. He wanted a fire that would spring to life full blown. One that would attack the area from several directions at once. He was sure he would be able to wipe out the Highlands, but he only wanted to use the community as a springboard to set Malibu, Santa Monica, and even Westwood—where his mom had died—ablaze.

Mark turned off Sunset Boulevard and drove into the valley. Because the area was exclusive and wealthy, security was strict. He had counted four private security patrol cars prowling the neighborhood at one time. It was common for one cruiser to be parked on Palisades Drive, the main road leading into the valley. Mark knew his gasoline truck would attract attention. To deflect it, he slowed as he neared the car and waved. Casually he rolled down his window.

"Do you know how to get to Michael Lane?" he asked.

The guard was reading a paperback. Was that all late-night employees ever did? He gestured up the road, hardly taking his eyes off the book. Mark knew the guy would not be able to identify him later, not that he really cared. Mark was having trouble thinking beyond that night.

"Take the road past the deli to the left, then take the first right," the guard said.

"Thanks," Mark called.

Off Michael Lane, behind a row of houses and condos, was the central fire road that the city had constructed to fight fires in the Pacific Palisades and Malibu hills. Mark found it ironic that he would use the road against the authorities. But as he parked at the flimsy gate that guarded the wide dirt path, he realized that he didn't have his lighter. He didn't even have matches; they were back in his car. He couldn't believe that he had overlooked such a simple necessity. Surely, if he left the valley in his gasoline truck and then turned around and came back minutes later, he would stir even the dull guard's curiosity. Yet to walk to his house from the Highlands would take longer than he had.

The solution to his dilemma presented itself a minute later when he spotted a bike parked beside a house. He felt bad about stealing it, but figured that since it would probably be molten steel in an hour, it didn't matter anyway. The bike afforded him more than transportation back to his house. He could pedal off the main fire road onto a narrow path and get back to his house without having to ride back down Palisades Drive. The private guard didn't have to see him again.

Mark was shocked to discover how hard it was to bike up the fire road. He was a strong hiker, but couldn't find the right combination of muscles and gears to make the climb on the bike any less laborious. He was drenched in sweat by the time he reached the narrow dirt path and started to coast downhill. He checked his watch: three-fifteen A.M. The fire had to start soon if it was to cause the most damage. Mark knew there were fire alerts all around the city at this time of the year, but he also knew that even firefighters were vulnerable in the early morning hours when they were sleepy.

It was only when he was within a half mile of his house that he thought of the people he might kill. Murder was not his intention—he had never hurt anyone before. In fact, he had gone out of his way to make sure no one was within range of his fiery hobby. But tonight he was contemplating the total destruction of at least one entire neighborhood. If he were honest with himself, he had to admit people were going to die. He planned to encircle the Highlands with flames, so complete evacuation would be impossible. Palisades Drive would be jammed with cars and the flames would sweep down. Thousands might die—it was possible. He understood that for a fact and yet he still planned to go ahead.

How unlike the Mark Charm he knew. But that was the question, wasn't it? Who was he really? MAZE had given him a glimpse into a fresh reality. His mother's death had given him a vision of an ancient horror. Lost somewhere between the two he operated outside the boundaries of his normal conscience. Once again he was struck by how his feelings did not seem to belong to him. Certainly he didn't even want to acknowledge these feelings; the prospect of the burning brought him no pleasure.

He couldn't stop thinking about the weird aliens on the stay-high TV channel. The disembodied brains floating in the blue fluid. The dreams that were only subconscious frustrations. The nightmares that would never end. He felt as if he were caught in a surreal drama that fit no physical stage. He needed to hurt people but didn't want them to suffer. The fire would come and he would be its instrument, but more than anything else he wanted to lie down on cool sheets and slip into peaceful oblivion. He felt powerless to contain what was happening inside him and wondered if he was possessed. Not for the first time, he wondered if Jessa really was a witch.

He was surprised to find her sitting on his porch.

She didn't seem surprised and studied him for a moment before saying, "I was worried about you."

He let the bike fall on his front yard. "How long have you been here?"

She shrugged. "Does it matter?" Her gaze narrowed. "Something's wrong."

He shook his head. "No, I'm fine. Look, can we talk tomorrow?"

She stood and moved to his side. "Tell me, Mark."

He couldn't look at her. The lump in his throat was a grenade. If he dropped the pin, it would shatter them both. Just then he felt his mother's death like an open wound. Wasn't that one rule of the game? Mothers died, every child in the world had to face that. It was all a question of timing— was the child young or old? A part of him felt as if he were still inside his mother's womb where it was dark but not warm. No soothing blood flowed around his undeveloped form. No rhythmic heart sang him to sleep. His mother was a lifeless manne- quin, whom they would bury soon. He kept wish- ing he had never been born and didn't understand why Jessa was trying to hug him. Her concern could not help him. Love was a worse curse; it was only because he had loved his mother so much that he suffered.

"She died, didn't she?" Jessa asked.

Mark stared. "Yes. She died."

Jessa buried her face in his chest. "I'm so sorry."

He held her at arm's length. "Why are you sorry?" There had been an odd note in her voice. She shook her head as if to say she didn't under- stand.

"I know how much she meant to you," she said. "You must be going through hell."

"Why did you leave while I was asleep?"

"I wanted you to rest."

"But why didn't you wake me?" he persisted.

She spoke carefully. "I don't know. Are you upset with me because of that? Had I awakened you, would you have been there in time to say goodbye to your mother?"

He turned away. "It doesn't matter."

She refused to let go of him. "Mark, you have to talk to me. You have to let me help you."

He snorted. "How do you want to help me? Give me another dose of MAZE?"

She paused. "If that's what you want. I'll give you anything I have."

He looked at her. "In exchange for what?"

Again, she acted confused. "I only want to be with you."

"Why? I mean the question seriously. We hardly know each other, and yet you're willing to do anything to help me. I don't get it."

She placed the palm of her hand against his chest. "I can't explain it, but I feel as if we have known each other for a long time. I mean it, you're not just a one-night stand to me."

He smiled thinly. "So we did have sex? I can't even remember. What does that say about our relationship? We have to get high to get close."

She continued to touch him. "I am always high around you."

He brushed her hand away. "You don't even know me!"

She stared. "Yes. I know you."

He turned his back on her. "Go away, Jessa. I'm very tired."

Her voice was soft. "But you're not going to sleep now. You have something you have to do first."

She said it with such certainty.

"Really?" he said.

She brought her mouth close to his ear. "You smell like gasoline."

"I stopped and got gas."

"In your electric Saturn?"

He glanced over his shoulder. "What's your point?"

She gestured back the way he had come. "Is your car over there? Or is it something else?"

He realized with a force that almost knocked him off his feet that she knew he was a pyromaniac. But how? Had he spoken to her of his perverse hobby while he had been on MAZE? That was the only explanation, but somehow he didn't think it was the right one. He turned to face her.

"What do you think it is?" he asked.

She was thoughtful. "Well, I think you are very upset, and that when you get this way you do strange things." She paused. "You have gasoline all over you."

"You said that already. What sort of strange things do I do when I am upset?"

She was so close he could feel the warmth of her breath on his cheek. She was so beautiful that even when he was angry with her it wasn't easy to forget her beauty. Her gray eyes shimmered in the glow from the street lamp. Or perhaps it was a spotlight cast on her from above, on Ebo, who was fated to die in the arms of her lover. Yet he was more worried about himself than he was about her as she lightly brushed her lips over his. She tasted like the fire he longed to create. He wondered if—long ago, in a world forgotten—she had placed the fire in him.

"You burn things," she whispered.

He was beyond stunned. "How do you know that?"

"I know you."

"But how?"

She hugged him. "I know because I love you."

He could not escape her embrace. Perhaps they would die in each other's arms. He had planned to set his fire and observe its destruction alone, but now he knew she would be with him when the flames of his madness swept down from the hills. His plans would have to expand and take caution into account. He could not kill her, nor could he destroy himself—not yet, not until he understood the nature of the spell she had cast over him.

5

They were in the truck high on the ridge, staring down at the sleeping houses, a three-mile trail of gasoline below them, pop waiting for corn, a party about to happen. Mark, Jessa by his side, had driven the fire road in the truck after taking his mom's car back to the truck. The hose was twisted at an angle so that the shrubs adjacent to the path would be sprayed. He had adjusted the valve to a narrow stream, calculating that it would be enough to ignite the dry growth. But now he worried that he had stretched his trail too far and thin. He needed the entire three miles to ignite. If there was a gap in the line, his plan would fail.

This was a plan? he asked himself. He still couldn't understand what drove him. Why couldn't he burn down a single house—or even a department store—like a normal pyromaniac? In his heart he felt the big barbecue would do nothing to soothe his pain. Why didn't he just go home to bed and sleep beside Jessa? She was weird; she knew more than a normal person, but she was still sexy. She could not erase his loss, but he suspected she could dull its bitter edge.

Yet he wouldn't stop. His momentum was too great and he couldn't even remember getting a running start. He had to do it because he had to do it. There was no why, only when. *Now* he climbed down from the front seat of the truck. He had his lighter, an old friend. Jessa watched him through the open door, from the passenger seat. Perhaps she thought he would lose his nerve.

"How many times have you done this?" she asked.

He shrugged. "I don't remember."

"How many big fires have you lit? A house or larger?"

He thought. "Five."

She was impressed. "Cool."

He was disturbed. "Don't you think I'm crazy?"

She shook her head. "Normal doesn't exist. It's just a term made up by stiff people."

He nodded at the sleeping valley. Black sky hugged the eastern horizon. The sun would rise in forty minutes, and he thought of the thousands who slept below him.

"People will die if I light this gasoline," he said.

She wasn't fazed. "No one is going to get hurt."

"How do you know that? What makes you an expert?"

"They'll evacuate before the flames reach them."

The wind tugged at his shirt. He fingered the lighter in his right palm. Even in the dry air, he was sweating. If anything the wind seemed to be picking up strength, blowing down the hill away from the path. They would be safe if the wind didn't suddenly change direction. Yet he knew it could do that—he was the real expert.

"I doubt it," he said, and sighed. He had pulled the truck several yards forward, from the end of the gasoline trail. It wouldn't do to explode their source of transportation back to his mom's car. He nodded to Jessa and walked back down the trail.

The smell of gasoline was thick. Yet this night it brought him no pleasure. There was too much of it, enough to drown in. He knelt at the end of his wet line and flicked his lighter. The orange flame danced in the harsh wind. How odd, he thought, that such a tiny beginning could create such a huge and tragic end. No wonder the ancients had worshipped fire. To Mark there could be no greater magic.

He lit the gasoline-dampened grass, the dead bushes.

As they began to burn, he stood and stepped back.

The fire moved faster than he could have imagined possible. Once again he was struck by the spirit it possessed. It took joy in its birth and wanted to touch as much as possible in its short life. Mark watched as the line of flames moved away from him and around the bend in the dirt path.

But there, abruptly, it halted.

He had made a mistake. The trail of gasoline must have been interrupted at that spot. True, the flames would cross the gap in a matter of minutes—and start the line again—but the power of surprise would be lost. The gap was only two hundred yards away. The wind pressed the existing flames off the path. He decided to run back and reestablish the line. He figured it would take him only a minute or two.

He didn't stop to tell Jessa his plan.

Mark was an excellent sprinter. His speed served him well on the tennis court, and when he was running from his fires. The smoke didn't bother him, his lungs almost preferred it to oxygen. He reached the gap in half a minute and knelt to find where the gasoline had run out. He had the nose for combustibles. He lit a bush and the fire line gained new life and raced around the next curve, a quarter mile distant.

There it stopped again.

"This is getting ridiculous," Mark muttered.

He knew he should turn back. It was the sensible thing to do, and even for a raving lunatic, he had

CHRISTOPHER PIKE

some common sense. The flames at his back were
gaining in strength. He hadn't parked the truck that
far from the start of his line and needed to alert
Jessa to the situation. If she could drive the truck a
mere hundred yards forward, he would feel more
comfortable about trying to correct the second gap
in the line.

Yet he didn't believe she was in any immediate
danger. The direction of the wind favored them
both. The natural inclination of the flames to
climb was suppressed by the blistering Santa
Anas. Mark decided to make a dash for it. With
the heat from the flames, his adrenaline had been
ignited. He felt a brush of mysterious power. As
Ray Bradbury had once said, it was a pleasure to
burn.

He didn't reach the second gap. A sixth sense
made him stop two-thirds of the way there. Less
than a minute had elapsed since he had checked the
flames closest to Jessa, but he knew he had to check
them again. What his eyes told him stopped him in
his latest rush. The wind had shifted north, back in
the direction of the truck. Crimson light played on
the steel hull of the now empty tank. He couldn't
see Jessa, probably she couldn't see the approaching fire. Raw panic shook his limbs.

But he wasn't normal. A switch deep inside his
brain must have shorted at birth. He didn't immediately scream to his girl and race back to the truck

70

to rescue her. He couldn't because the line of fire had not been completed. Even as he reeled at the thought of what would happen if the fire touched the vapors in the empty tank, he turned his back on Jessa. The gap had to be filled, the destruction had to be complete. The aliens understood. Perhaps it was he, and not Jessa, who was the visitor to this world. He felt superhuman—felt he could master the fire and save his girl all in the same precious seconds.

Mark focused his attention on the fire. It was as if his forehead pulsed with a magnetic power that helped push the fire onto fresh fuel. The flames danced around the next bend and the one beyond that. Half the valley was encircled in fire. Yet again another break in the line occurred; he saw the flames stall on the far side of the hills. He stared at it intently, praying for a thunderbolt from Zeus to restart it. The wind and smoke tore at his damp eyes. His head ached. The fire did jump then as if whipped, and the gap vanished as the line of flame raced for the finish line. Finally the valley was enclosed; only one road could lead its inhabitants to safety.

Mark turned back to the truck.

Jessa stood outside it on the dirt path, a slash of cool in an insane inferno. It could have been a trick of the light, but it seemed as if her gray eyes were magnified in the intense heat and silently pleaded to him for help. But did he feel her fears or curse his own? She didn't move away from the truck even as the flames came near. He frantically waved his arms and ran toward her.

"Get away from the truck!" he screamed.

She must not have heard him. She made no move to save herself. Perhaps she believed the empty tank was not volatile, when in fact it was more likely to explode than a full tank. It was the fumes that burned, not the liquid. Mark doubted that Jessa had taken chemistry. She was not that kind of girl. She was a witch, and she must have thought the fire could not touch her.

The truck exploded.

The ball of orange light expanded slowly. Mark saw Jessa lifted off her feet and shoved to one side, a cartoon figure on a deranged screen. For a moment she was suspended in midair—the fire a part of her aura, blazing with a heavenly radiance. Not for a second did he think she would survive the blast. She hit the ground, on the far side of the fire road, and bounced two times before coming to rest. Her clothes were on fire.

She was still burning when Mark reached her— her pants, the hem of her blouse. After stripping off his shirt, he smothered the flames and rolled her onto her back. Her hair and face appeared untouched. The hills blazed all around them. They would both be consumed if they didn't move in the next minute. Jessa opened her eyes and smiled up at him.

"Wow," she said.

Hope burst in his chest. He had been sure he was extinguishing a corpse. He knelt by her side and cradled her head in his lap.

"How do you feel?" he asked.

Sweat poured over her red face. Everything was red, the explosion could have blown them both to hell. "Hot," she said.

His voice cracked. "I thought you were dead."

She did not tease. "I cannot die."

Mark glanced around anxiously. Their transportation was gone and the wind was howling. The trick was to move opposite to the way it was blowing. That meant going up and over the hill, to higher ground. He had never carried a person before, certainly not someone who was seriously wounded. Jessa acted brave, but it was clear she could not walk. He doubted she felt the burns yet. But later, if she survived, she would feel them more than she had ever felt anything. Guilt threatened to paralyze him, but he fought against it. He leaned over and gripped her back and hips.

"I'm going to put you over my shoulders," he said. "We're going to get out of here."

She nodded. "I trust you."

Perhaps it was because of the desperate nature of their situation—and his pounding adrenaline—

but she did not feel that heavy. He worried that he would be able to carry her only a few feet, but he bounded up the side of the hill at a strong pace. The wind pressed against his face, the fire fell behind.

Unfortunately, they had no clear escape route. He wouldn't be able to carry her the miles required to get them out of the hills. If anything they were moving farther away from civilization, and the wind could turn again at any second. He briefly considered stopping and waiting for the fire to take them. One thing for sure, he was not going to leave her to save himself.

She must have read his mind.

"You can't carry me forever," she mumbled beside his head.

"Sure I can. Just relax."

She coughed. The smoke was chasing them even if the fire was not.

"My legs hurt," she said.

He panted. "You're lucky to be alive."

"I'm lucky you're here."

"Yeah. I'm the one who got us into this mess."

"No," she said quietly. "It was me."

He didn't understand what she meant. It didn't matter. As he crested the bluff he saw that the fire had already spread to the far side of the hill, the wind now working against them. They were surrounded on three sides, so he pushed toward the

ne did not feel that heavy. He worried that he
d be able to carry her only a few feet, but he
ded up the side of the hill at a strong pace
wind pressed against his face, the fire fel
d.

fortunately, they had no clear escape route
ouldn't be able to carry her the miles required
t them out of the hills. If anything they were
ng farther away from civilization, and the
 could turn again at any second. He briefly
dered stopping and waiting for the fire to take
. One thing for sure, he was not going to leave
o save himself.

e must have read his mind.

ou can't carry me forever," she mumbled
e his head.

re I can. Just relax."

e coughed. The smoke was chasing them even
 fire was not.

y legs hurt," she said.

 panted. "You're lucky to be alive."

m lucky you're here."

eah. I'm the one who got us into this mess."

o," she said quietly. "It was me."

didn't understand what she meant. It didn't
r. As he crested the bluff he saw that the fire
lready spread to the far side of the hill, the
now working against them. They were sur-
led on three sides, so he pushed toward the

to rescue her. He couldn't because the line of fire had not been completed. Even as he reeled at the thought of what would happen if the fire touched the vapors in the empty tank, he turned his back on Jessa. The gap had to be filled, the destruction had to be complete. The aliens understood. Perhaps it was he, and not Jessa, who was the visitor to this world. He felt superhuman—felt he could master the fire and save his girl all in the same precious seconds.

Mark focused his attention on the fire. It was as if his forehead pulsed with a magnetic power that helped push the fire onto fresh fuel. The flames danced around the next bend and the one beyond that. Half the valley was encircled in fire. Yet again another break in the line occurred; he saw the flames stall on the far side of the hills. He stared at it intently, praying for a thunderbolt from Zeus to restart it. The wind and smoke tore at his damp eyes. His head ached. The fire did jump then as if whipped, and the gap vanished as the line of flame raced for the finish line. Finally the valley was enclosed; only one road could lead its inhabitants to safety.

Mark turned back to the truck.

Jessa stood outside it on the dirt path, a slash of cool in an insane inferno. It could have been a trick of the light, but it seemed as if her gray eyes were magnified in the intense heat and silently pleaded to him for help. But did he feel her fears or curse his own? She didn't move away from the truck even as the flames came near. He frantically waved his arms and ran toward her.

"Get away from the truck!" he screamed.

She must not have heard him. She made no move to save herself. Perhaps she believed the empty tank was not volatile, when in fact it was more likely to explode than a full tank. It was the fumes that burned, not the liquid. Mark doubted that Jessa had taken chemistry. She was not that kind of girl. She was a witch, and she must have thought the fire could not touch her.

The truck exploded.

The ball of orange light expanded slowly. Mark saw Jessa lifted off her feet and shoved to one side, a cartoon figure on a deranged screen. For a moment she was suspended in midair—the fire a part of her aura, blazing with a heavenly radiance. Not for a second did he think she would survive the blast. She hit the ground, on the far side of the fire road, and bounced two times before coming to rest. Her clothes were on fire.

She was still burning when Mark reached her— her pants, the hem of her blouse. After stripping off his shirt, he smothered the flames and rolled her onto her back. Her hair and face appeared untouched. The hills blazed all around them. They would both be consumed if they didn't move in the

next minute. Jessa opened her eye at him.

"Wow," she said.

Hope burst in his chest. He had b extinguishing a corpse. He knelt b cradled her head in his lap.

"How do you feel?" he asked.

Sweat poured over her red face. red, the explosion could have blown hell. "Hot," she said.

His voice cracked. "I thought you She did not tease. "I cannot die."

Mark glanced around anxiously. tation was gone and the wind was trick was to move opposite to th blowing. That meant going up and higher ground. He had never ca before, certainly not someone who wounded. Jessa acted brave, but it could not walk. He doubted she fel But later, if she survived, she would than she had ever felt anything. Gui paralyze him, but he fought agains over and gripped her back and hip

"I'm going to put you over my said. "We're going to get out of her

She nodded. "I trust you."

Perhaps it was because of the des their situation—and his poundin fourth—down the north side of the ridge. He vaguely remembered a huge drainage pipe jutting out from the side of the hill. To get to it he suspected they would have to walk through fire, but figured they had no choice. The entire hilltop would burn, the drain would be their only chance at shelter.

Finally the wind gave them a break. It shifted slightly to the south and they had enough breathing room to be able to move into the wide gully that would eventually become the affluent valley. Off to his left he could see that the fire had already reached a large house. The Mercedes-Benz parked out in front exploded and people ran screaming down the block. Yet for Mark the distant scene was surreal—film on a holographic screen. Only Jessa lying over his shoulder mattered. She moaned softly.

Where the hell was that drain?

"Sore," Jessa whispered.

"We're almost there," he promised.

"Where?"

"A place to rest."

She breathed. "Good."

He didn't see the drain, he stumbled over it. That was because its opening was three-quarters buried by bushes and shrubs. He set Jessa down and clawed at the dry branches. The fire had claimed the hill above; it was coming down into the gully. His plan had worked too well. The flames were spreading in every direction. Far off he heard the shouts of terrified people. Palisades Drive was probably already jammed.

"It'll be cool inside this drain," he said to Jessa. Sweat stung his eyes. The temperature had to be over 120°, and it was getting harder to breathe. His coughing made the digging harder. He realized he wasn't going to get all the debris out of the way—they'd have to squeeze past it. Returning to Jessa, he explained the situation, but he was talking to himself. Jessa had blacked out.

Mark decided to squeeze inside the drain first, to clear a path for Jessa. The fire was fifty feet away. One sharp gust in their direction and they'd be buried in orange pain. He stuck his head in the drain and reached out to feel for any kind of grip. There was a crack in the pipe ceiling. He used it to pull himself through a mass of tangled weeds. All the way inside, he turned back for Jessa and hoped the drain went back far into the hill and had air-conditioning.

Jessa was still unconscious. He grabbed her by the ankles and pulled her toward the drain. Her head smacked a large stone and he cursed himself a thousand times. Her burnt skin beneath his fingers felt like raw hamburger. Stretching back like a yogi doing a posture, he pushed off with his feet, pulling Jessa with him. Sharp sticks and pebbles tore at the exposed skin on his back. He kept inching backward, sure he was destroying Jessa's skin for life.

When they were all the way inside, the temperature dropped and Mark was able to catch his breath. The drain was five feet in diameter, designed for the runoff from winter floods. Mark twisted around and crawled back so his head was beside Jessa's. He was surprised that her eyes were open. The fire moved close to the drain entrance. Still, they had cool air flowing at their backs. He realized the pipe must exit on the far side of the hills.

"How do you feel?" he asked as he stroked her damp cheek.

She coughed weakly. "I'm OK."

He glanced down the black tunnel. "We can't stay here. The smoke will thicken and we'll suffocate. We have to get to the other end of this drain. But I can't carry you in here. Do you think you can crawl?"

She forced a smile. "I can fly."

His question had been foolish. She was barely conscious. "I screwed up," he said, pain in his voice.

She reached up and brushed his hair aside. "You did what you had to do."

He shook his head. "How can you say that? I've killed us both."

She pulled his head closer. "No," she whispered. "Leave me, I'll be all right."

The fire beat at their open door. The temperature swelled back up. Smoke poured into the metal shaft, and they both began to choke.

"I leave you and you die," he said.

Her expression was peaceful. "I told you, I'm immortal. Please, save yourself, Mark."

Outside the wind howled like a disembodied spirit. Perhaps it had given them a reprieve only to lengthen their torture. Flames licked at the edge of the metal drain. The heat from the fire blistered the skin on his bare chest. Every instinct in his body screamed for him to turn and crawl deeper into the tunnel. Instead he grabbed Jessa by the shoulders and tried to yank her body around.

"I can save us both," he said frantically. "A hundred feet inside and the smoke won't kill us."

She stopped him. "I can't move. It hurts too much."

He wept. "But I can't leave you! Jessa! You've got to try!"

She shook her head sadly. "No, I'll stay here. I have to stay here. Everything will be OK."

He understood that she couldn't move if she wanted to. Since he wouldn't leave her, there was nothing more to discuss. Smoke filled the tunnel like fog descending. Mark stretched out and lay down beside her. The flames could not touch them, but the superheated air would kill them just the same. Every inhalation was thick with gases. But through it all Jessa shivered and never lost her peaceful smile. It was one more mystery he would never understand about her.

"This was meant to happen," she said.

It was the last words he heard.

The fire came near. The Magic Fire.

6

Mark awoke to the sound of his own coughing
and a torturous pain in his right arm. There was
no transition—he was unconscious one minute
and then fully alert the next. He sat up and looked
around. He was in a king-size bed in a luxurious
penthouse, Jessa asleep or knocked out beside
him. An IV led into her right arm and both her
legs were heavily bandaged. She wore a short
white slip, nothing else. He had on white under-
wear that didn't belong to him. His right arm had
been professionally bandaged from the wrist to
the biceps. His left arm was also burned but not so
badly. A greasy ointment had been smeared on the
reddened flesh. The remainder of him had been
scrubbed clean. The act of washing him had not
awakened him—he found that curious, along with
other things.

Mark got out of bed and walked to the windows and pulled aside the heavy drapes. The view outside shocked him. He knew immediately that he must be atop one of the downtown L.A. skyscrapers. It was night but he knew it could not be the same night. Yet, far away on the West Side, fires continued to burn. It looked as if all of Santa Monica were on fire, and probably Pacific Palisades and Malibu as well. The intervening hills made the latter assumption hard to verify. A ghastly red glow dominated the horizon—nuclear holocaust courtesy of one well-placed lighter.

He felt such shame.

His arm was killing him and he had to pee. Quietly slipping into the bathroom, he discovered a gray robe and sandals waiting for him on the sink counter. There was also a bottle of prescription medicine—Percocet. His mother had taken the powerful painkiller before she had graduated to even stronger drugs. He studied the bottle—the prescription written by a Dr. Brain was made out to him. He debated the wisdom of taking a pill for a moment. Whatever was happening was weird beyond belief. He needed his senses sharp, but the pain was driving him crazy. He swallowed one pill with a glass of water, and knew it would be twenty minutes before the drug kicked in. He could hardly wait. He hoped Jessa was well medicated.

Careful not to wet his bandage, Mark took a

shower. He had been cleaned up, but there was a faint aroma of smoke in his hair, which was making him slightly nauseated. While standing under the running water he felt slightly detached from his throbbing arm—the Percocet must be working faster than he had imagined. By the time he was dried and dressed in the robe, he felt little pain.

He was suddenly starving and remembered seeing a refrigerator in the corner of the bedroom. After tiptoeing out of the bathroom, he was pleased to discover the icebox contained fresh turkey, whole wheat bread, and plenty of lettuce, tomatoes, and mayonnaise—fixings for a great sandwich. There was also apple juice and a large bag of potato chips. He worried that his eating would disturb Jessa, but he was beginning to realize she was knocked out. He made two sandwiches and wolfed them, washing them down with a quart of apple juice. He felt terribly dehydrated and wondered how long he had been unconscious.

It was odd, but while he was doing all these things, he never thought to explore beyond the bedroom door. But now that he was pain free and no longer starving, he tried the brass handle and was surprised to find it unlocked. It led into a well-furnished living room with a glorious view of the city. Of course all the windows looked west, in the direction of the fires, which were out of control.

Smoke blanketed the city. He wondered how extensive the damage would be. Most of all, he worried how many had died.

He tried the penthouse front door. Locked.

Who had rescued them?

There was a large TV and remote in the corner of the living room. Mark turned it on and sat on a richly upholstered sofa. The news stations were focused exclusively on the fires. Two hundred people were already reported dead, one newscaster said, but the toll would surely be many times that. Property damage was impossible to estimate—it would be at least a hundred billion. Santa Monica was partially damaged but Malibu and Pacific Palisades were furnaces. Pepperdine College had been burned to the ground and from aerial shots it was clear that the Highlands had been obliterated—not a single house stood. Firefighters blamed the intense winds and the magnitude of the fire on their inability to contain it. There was no relief in sight.

Mark bowed his head and wept.

There was a knock at the front door.

Mark stood quickly and turned off the set.

No one walked in, so he had to call out.

"Yes?" he said.

The door opened and in walked a man dressed entirely in black. Mark had only glimpsed the guy the night he had burned down the house in the

Malibu hills—the last night of Jessa's play—but he recognized him nevertheless. Mark wasn't surprised to see him because he felt he had been *followed* since that evening. On the other hand, nothing that was happening was logical, and Mark felt trapped in a disjointed play. He kept waiting for the audience to applaud or someone to bring down the curtain. He wanted to draw the drapes, to shut out the view of the fires. He was sure the man knew who had started them.

Yet there was no sign of judgment on the man's face. He could have been a flesh and blood robot, a creature of the future—his impassiveness was masklike, calm and indifferent. His age was a mystery. Although deeply tanned, he had no wrinkles, and his narrow black eyes were stonelike and never blinking. His lips were thin and leatherlike, his forehead massive—a reservoir of intelligence, crowned with thick bronze hair. His powerful build was clad in a well-cut black suit. He didn't look as if he had to work out to maintain his physique. A force of nature, he radiated authority in every step. He didn't need to speak to intimidate Mark.

His voice, when he finally spoke, was surprisingly soothing.

"How are you feeling, Mark?" he asked.

"Fine." Mark cleared his throat. "Who are you?"

"My name is Mr. Grimes." The man moved

farther into the penthouse and gestured to a chair. "May I?"

"Sure." Mark nervously sat down on the couch. The distant fires continued to burn. He gestured to his bandaged arm. "Did you do this?"

Mr. Grimes spoke politely. "An associate of mine."

"Dr. Brain?"

"Precisely."

"What kind of name is that?" Mark asked.

Mr. Grimes was diplomatic. "What's on your mind, son?"

"Who you are—besides your name? What do you want with me and Jessa? How did we come to be rescued? Small details like that."

Mr. Grimes stared at the fires before answering. At first he had appeared to be invincible, and even though Mark continued to sense his strength, he was now aware that the man carried heavy burdens. Mr. Grimes sighed before responding.

"What I am going to tell you now is not the whole truth. It is a portion of it, a true portion, but necessarily incomplete. I am here to win your confidence. I do not believe I can lie to you and accomplish that. Naturally, when I am finished speaking you will ask why I cannot tell you more. Let me say at the start that I am not the final word when it comes to you. There exists a group above me, a powerful group, that dictates much of my actions." Mr. Grimes paused. "Do you understand?"

"No, but please go on. Why am I here?"

"You are here because my associates and I saved your life. You have been under observation for some time—since your father died in fact." He paused. "Do you remember your father?"

"He died when I was ten. I remember him, but only from a kid's perspective." Mark shrugged. "He was a nice man."

"Do you miss him?"

"I would like to say I do but I honestly don't. Why?"

"I am merely curious. Do you know how he died?"

"In an accident, in a fire."

"Where?"

Mark swallowed. "I believe it was a fire in the Malibu hills."

Mr. Grimes gestured to the windows. "Those same hills are burning now, eight years later."

Mark fidgeted. "It was an accident."

Mr. Grimes raised an eyebrow. He remained outwardly impassive, but Mark had the impression that his every word was carefully calculated for its effect—that their meeting was the culmination of many years of planning by the man. Mark struggled to understand why these people would have had him under observation for nearly a decade.

"Now or then?" Mr. Grimes asked.

"What's your point?"

"The fires that burn now were not accidentally set. You started them on purpose. Your father also started the fire that killed him, but he did so unintentionally, and—in a subtle way—so did you."

Mark tensed. "My father was not a pyromaniac. He died a hero. He was awarded a medal posthumously by the mayor of the city."

"He was indeed awarded such a medal. My associates and I attended the ceremony, and his funeral as well. Your father probably died thinking he was a hero, but he also died knowing he was a pyromaniac. He loved to be close to fires, which is why he chose the work he did. But I believe he kept his desire in check, most of his life, better than you have. Still, he did cause the fire that killed him."

Mark struggled. "I don't understand."

"Have you heard the term *pyrokinesis?*"

"Yes. It refers to the ability to start a fire with one's mind. . . ." Mark stopped. "No—you don't know what you're talking about—"

"But I do, we have watched your family for many years, more than you can imagine. Your father was able to start fires with his mind. Most of your ancestors had the same ability." Mr. Grimes paused. "You have it as well, Mark."

Mark snorted. "Right. Then why did I need a gasoline truck and a lighter to get this inferno started?"

"Let me answer your question with a question. When the line of fire stalled in the Highlands, a mile from where you were standing, how did you restart it?"

"It restarted by itself."

"How?" Mr. Grimes asked.

"The fire jumped the gap in the line, as you would expect it to."

"And when it did this, at that exact moment, you felt nothing unusual?"

"No," Mark said quickly.

"You answer defensively. There is nothing shameful in your ability. Pause and reconsider. Did you feel anything strange at the moment the fire jumped the gap?"

"No."

"You are not being honest with yourself."

Mark was annoyed. "How do you know what I felt? You can't read my mind."

The comment hung in the air. Mr. Grimes smiled faintly, and Mark had to wonder if the guy *could* read his mind. But Mr. Grimes's smile was short-lived; it faded as he stared out the window.

"How do you feel about the damage you've caused?" Mr. Grimes asked.

Mark spoke softly. "Not good."

"And Jessa? What you have done to her?"

Mark lowered his head. "Will she be all right?"

"She is badly burned. Even with the best medical attention, she will be scarred for life."

Mark thought of her soft skin, of her lying in bed beside him, telling him her secret story, her mysterious tale that he couldn't remember now. He found it hard to breathe.

"Shouldn't she be in a hospital?" he mumbled.

Mr. Grimes leaned forward. "We can do more for her than a hospital can." He removed what looked like a tube of toothpaste from his pocket. "Come here, remove your bandage."

"What?" Mark asked.

"Do as I say; don't be afraid."

Mark stood and slowly picked at his bandage. Even with the Percocet in his veins, it was painful to touch. Mr. Grimes gestured him closer, took Mark's right arm, and yanked at the bandage, tearing it free. Agony shot up Mark's arm and socked his brain. Stars swam in his vision as he almost passed out. He tried not to look at the blistered skin, but he was too late. From wrist to biceps, his flesh was a mass of pus and ruined tissue. The narcotic had fooled him into thinking he was not seriously hurt. He needed to get to a hospital as well.

Mr. Grimes opened his unmarked tube of white

CHRISTOPHER PIKE

cream. He continued to grip Mark's arm; he was a strong S.O.B. "Relax, be still," Mr. Grimes said gently.

Mark trembled. "What are you doing?"

"Your pain will be over in a minute." Squeezing a small amount of the cream onto his fingertip, Mr. Grimes massaged it into the skin above Mark's wrist. At first Mark recoiled from the treatment, but almost immediately he felt a decrease in sensation in the area. He watched amazed as Mr. Grimes rubbed the cream over the remainder of his arm. Not only was the pain decreasing, the redness and blisters were healing as well. But that was impossible, Mark thought, medical science had not advanced to the point where it could instantly remove a burn. Three minutes after starting the treatment, Mark felt no pain at all. His skin appeared to be almost normal. Mr. Grimes released him and gestured to Mark's left arm.

"Would you like some there as well?" he asked.

Mark drew back and felt his arm. His head spun with the impossibility of the miracle he had just witnessed. "Who are you?" he demanded.

"I told you."

"You told me nothing! You bring Jessa and me to this place, and lock us inside, and tell me that I am some kind of fire freak from a race of fire freaks. Then you work some kind of hocus-pocus on my

90

arm. And you say you are here to win my confidence? You are blowing my mind, that's what you're doing." He stopped. "I want to get out of here."

Mr. Grimes indicated the front door. "It is no longer locked. You are free to leave."

Mark took a step toward the door, stopped. "I can't leave without Jessa."

"Fine. Take her with you."

Mark was bitter. "You know I can't do that. She can't leave here without an ambulance."

"Call one then. There is a phone in the bedroom."

Mark pointed to the tube of cream. "She needs that!"

Mr. Grimes weighed the tube in his hand. "She can live without it."

Mark nodded darkly. "I see where you're heading. If I cooperate, Jessa gets the cream. Otherwise, you make her suffer."

Mr. Grimes was calm. "Who makes her suffer? Who started the fire?" He paused. "Sit down, Mark, you don't know what you're dealing with here."

Mark felt the strength drain from his body. He plopped back down on the couch. "All right, I'm listening," he muttered.

"You have to do more than listen. You have to acknowledge the validity of what I am saying.

Think back to last night, when you stood on the ridge and the line of fire failed. You wanted it to restart, it was important to you. Your girlfriend was in danger, but still you worried that the fire was incomplete. It is your nature to burn, Mark. That quality, that power, springs from deep inside you." He paused. "What did you feel at that moment?"

Mark considered. "A pressure in my head."

"What was it like?"

Mark sweated. It was almost as if he were standing on the ridge again, flames all around, smoke in his lungs, heat on his face. Mr. Grimes stared at him intensely, and it seemed to Mark that fire burned in the depths of the man as well. But his was a cold fire, and Mark realized that the only reason the guy was spending time with him was to get something from him. Otherwise, to Mr. Grimes he was nothing, a tool to use and discard.

"It felt magnetic, alive," Mark said. "It seemed to strike out from my forehead."

"When that happened, that strike, the fire restarted?"

What he said was true. Mark had not realized it before. "Yes."

Mr. Grimes sat back in his chair and pocketed the tube of cream. It was as if he had reached point A with Mark and would now move on to point B.

Mark felt he was being maneuvered, but the knowledge did not help because Mr. Grimes had all the answers. Yet the man needed Mark's fire-starting ability, that much was obvious.

"You may ask some questions," Mr. Grimes said.

"My father had this ability?"

"Yes."

"Did he know he had it?" Mark asked.

Mr. Grimes was thoughtful. "He suspected he had it. But certainly he had no conscious control of it. That is how he accidentally killed himself. He inadvertently fed the flames that destroyed him."

"Why would he do that?"

"I told you, it was his nature, as it is your nature. You burn, it is what you do."

"Who do you work for? The government?"

"No. Ours is a small but old organization."

"How old?" Mark asked.

"Very. Many centuries."

"No shit? What do you call yourselves?"

Mr. Grimes hesitated. "I am afraid that is one question I cannot answer. Simply accept that I and my associates are part of an ancient mystical order."

"Mystical?" That had been the last thing Mark expected to hear. "Can any of your people start fires with their minds?"

"Not as well as you can."

"That is why you need me?"

"Yes."

Mark took a breath. "OK. What do you need me for?"

"We need you as a weapon."

Once again, Mark was thrown off by the reply. "You want to use my ability to start a fire against somebody?"

"Yes."

"That's insane. OK, maybe there is something inside of me that allows me to start fires. I'm not sure of that, but I will take your word for it, for now. But surely my mind is not more powerful than conventional weapons."

Mr. Grimes considered. "We do not know the extent of your power, that is true. We hope to discover that in the next few days. But more important than the magnitude of your power is the nature of it. The enemy we wish to use it against does not know it exists."

"Who is this enemy?"

Mr. Grimes stared. "An alien race."

Mark burst out laughing. "Right. Now there are aliens. What's the matter, are they about to invade Earth?"

Mr. Grimes was unmoved. "They have already invaded Earth."

Mark kept laughing. "Really? God, I must have missed it somehow."

"Your sarcasm is understandable, but you will come to see that it is unwarranted. Few humans know that we have been invaded and conquered. The major governments of the world do not even know. Yet it is a fact, a provable fact."

Mark spread his hands. "All right, prove it to me."

"Not at this time. But later, before we ask you to use your ability against them, you will have proof of their existence."

Mark shook his head. "No deal. You make a ridiculous statement like that and you have to back it up immediately. I mean, how do I know that you and your ancient band of mystics are not refugees from a mental clinic?"

Mr. Grimes gestured. "There is the matter of your injured arm. You saw it heal before your eyes. Does that not prove to you that we know a thing or two?"

"No. It's an entirely different matter."

"But we also knew that you could start fires with your mind. How many others knew that?"

He had a point there. "Jessa knew," he muttered.

Mr. Grimes jerked slightly, uncharacteristically. "She told you that?"

"Not exactly. But she seems to know things about me that no one else does—at least not until you showed up." Mark paused. "Have you been observing her as well?"

Mr. Grimes considered. "She is of interest to us as well."

"Why?"

"I cannot tell you why."

"Why not?" Mark insisted.

"I have explained, my superiors dictate what I can and cannot say."

"I want to meet them."

"That is impossible. But trust that they are a wise group."

"I'm nowhere near having that level of trust in any of you." Mark shook his head again. "What are these aliens like?"

"They are humanoids. They look no different from you or me."

Mark snickered. "It figures."

"Why do you say that?"

"Isn't it obvious? Of course they look like you and me. Probably because they're not aliens."

"But they *are* aliens. They are from another star system."

"Which one?"

"It is named NCG123 in the star catalogs. It is located four hundred and twenty light-years from here."

"How did you know that? Did they tell you?"

"No. We have—spies."

Mark chuckled. "Like James Bond?"

"No. Our spies are like you in that they possess

unique mental abilities. They are able to view the aliens psychically. The aliens do not possess these same abilities. Even though their technology is advanced far beyond ours, they do not even suspect these abilities of yours exist. For that reason they are the prime instruments we can use against them."

"I don't believe you. I don't believe any of this."

"You will, in time."

Mark stood. "I won't be here—in time. I am leaving tonight, with Jessa. Are you going to give me that cream or not?"

"If you leave, no. If you stay, yes."

"That's blackmail."

"Call it what you wish. We need you, Mark, mankind needs you. Why not take a few days to see what this is about?"

"Because I can't stay here while those fires are burning out there!" Mark stabbed at the window and turned away. He trembled all over and couldn't stop. The guilt hit him again—it had never really left, and he worried it never would. He had killed people! His fire was killing them even as he remained in this fancy penthouse and argued with this insane man. He didn't know what to do, but he felt he had to do something to stop what he had started. But there was Jessa and her horrible burns . . . and Mr. Grimes speaking soothingly behind him.

"Tragic as these fires seem to you now, they will appear meaningless in a few days. What you can do for mankind will more than outweigh what you think you have done to them with your recklessness."

"What I *think* I have done to them?" Mark asked bitterly. "Have you not watched the news? I have murdered at least two hundred people."

Mr. Grimes stood. "You will soon see that our enemy has done far worse. The choice is yours— stay or leave." He stepped toward the door. "I will return in the morning."

Mark turned. "Jessa will wake soon. She will be in pain."

Mr. Grimes stopped at the door. "Give her a pill."

Mark was bitter. "You should leave the cream."

Mr. Grimes opened the door. "You should think about what I have said."

Mr. Grimes left. The door closed quietly behind him.

Mark returned to the bedroom. Jessa was sitting up and moaning, but she smiled when she saw him. "You saved us," she said.

Mark sat on the bed beside her and took her hand. "It wasn't me. Someone brought us here."

"Who?"

"It's a long story. Before I tell you, can you tell me if you have any psychic abilities?"

She wasn't as puzzled as he would have expected.

"Yes, I have one," she said. "I have a vivid imagination."

"No. I mean can you—"

She interrupted by putting a finger to his lips.

"Shh," she whispered. "My power is you, that I have you. That is all the power I need."

7

The next day Mr. Grimes and a muscle-bound associate took Mark and Jessa into the desert in a motor home. Mark and Jessa stayed in the back, as she had to remain lying down. As a sign of good faith—so Mark assumed—Mr. Grimes had treated Jessa's right leg with the cream, healed the damn thing in minutes. But he had done nothing for her left one and Mark feared the ruined flesh was rotting. It smelled under the thick bandages they had left in place. Jessa complained little, although it was obvious she was in tremendous pain. Mark marveled at her strength, that she even seemed to enjoy the ride in the motor home.

"I have always loved the desert," she explained when he remarked on her good cheer. There was a window beside the head of the bed, and she scanned the distant brown horizon as she spoke.

They were on Highway 15, rolling toward Las Vegas, but Mark knew that could not be their final destination. Mr. Grimes had spoken of a secret desert facility where Mark's abilities could be tested and improved. Jessa continued, "I used to drive out to the desert at night, and lie on my back, and stare up at the stars."

"What do you think of those same stars now?" Mark asked. He had told Jessa everything Mr. Grimes had said. He was still trying to sort out her reaction. It wasn't as if she believed the mysterious guy, but Mark was pretty sure she didn't disbelieve him, either. The prospect of being needed by an ancient order to save mankind seemed to thrill her. Plus having one of her legs healed didn't hurt much, either. Yet the fact that Mr. Grimes continued to make Jessa suffer galled Mark.

"I will always love the stars," Jessa said seriously, staring at him with her soulful gray eyes, which touched him deeper now because of the pain behind them. "Just because one star brought us woe doesn't mean that great things cannot come from the others."

Mark snorted. "I don't know."

"What don't you know?"

"I don't know anything, that's the problem. I am without a reference point." He stopped. "I watched the news this morning before we left."

Jessa reached for his hand. "Try not to think about it."

Mark shook his head. "Over four hundred dead and still the fire has not been contained. I'm almost glad my mother died when she did. It would have killed her to know what I've done."

"It would have made her proud to know that you are going to help billions of people."

"That is not real! None of this can be real!" Mark glanced toward the front of the motor home. The other two were out of sight, but he could nevertheless feel them watching and listening. "You've hardly spoken to Mr. Grimes. How can you trust him?"

She stroked his hand. "I didn't say I trusted him. I don't know what he is up to. But I trust you. I know you will do something great with what's inside you. I feel it in my heart."

"You hardly know me, Jessa."

They hit a bump. The motor home rattled. Jessa gasped in pain but covered it quickly. Mark reached for the bottle of Percocet, but she waved it away. She had been taking a pill every hour, a heavy dose. She really needed a hospital. No, she needed the cream, damn Mr. Grimes.

"I told you, I do know you," she said. "If you don't believe that, then we have nothing."

He could not take his eyes off her. "I want to believe you."

She smiled faintly. "I want you to kiss me."

He moved close. "I might hurt you."

"You can't hurt me."

He kissed her, and it hurt him, to feel her so close, so injured. He would have given his left leg to make hers whole again. But all he could do, according to Mr. Grimes, was burn. As he pulled back he ran a hand through her hair.

"I know what they want you for," he said.

"Leverage?"

"Perhaps. But they must know that you have magic. You're a healer, you've healed me."

His remark embarrassed her. She averted her gaze.

"I wasn't there for you when your mother died," she said.

"You were there."

"No." Her gaze came back to him. He was surprised to see a tear in her eye. "I wasn't there," she repeated.

"I wasn't there, either."

"Yes, you were."

"No."

She squeezed his hands and spoke with emotion. "Yes, Mark. Don't doubt it."

This was why he wanted to believe her. This was why it was hard. So much of what she said made no sense. Yet it rang true in a part of him that he felt he had somehow misplaced. It was as if the MAZE had never truly worn off. He thought of the aliens he had seen while on the drug, the transparent skulls, the disembodied brains floating in blue fluid. He picked up the bottle of Percocet and again noted the doctor's name on the prescription—Dr. Brain. Mr. Grimes said the man would be at the secret facility.

"We'll see," he whispered.

Thirty miles short of Las Vegas they turned off Highway 15 and headed north on a bumpy asphalt road that disintegrated into loose gravel and weeds. The rough going was hard on Jessa, and she ended up taking two more pills. Her eyes glazed over slightly and she eventually closed them and dosed. Mark tried to memorize the route, should he, say, want to escape from the facility in the middle of the night.

They didn't halt for over an hour. The compound came up abruptly, fenced-in buildings tucked between low-lying hills, with barbed wire around the perimeter. There was nobody in sight, but high-powered camera lenses guarded every corner. The gate opened automatically and the motor home rolled inside. The gate was closed before Mark climbed outside.

There were three single-story buildings, each identical, square brick affairs that somehow gave the impression of being facades. Mark suspected they contained multilevel basements, underground torture chambers. Not a single bush, plant, or blade of grass enhanced the grounds. The sand looked dry enough to swallow blood. The brickwork and roof tiles appeared fresh. Mark didn't understand how the government couldn't know such a place existed. It looked like a spy joint.

Mr. Grimes, still wearing his black suit, waited with Mark while the steroid-enhanced driver disappeared into the nearest building. He wore black as well, and Mark wondered if he was enlisting on the side of the good guys. The temperature was over a hundred.

"How is Jessa?" Mr. Grimes asked.

"She's asleep now, but she was in pain on the drive here. Why not help her out, huh?"

"Soon." Mr. Grimes remained cool in the blazing sun. "When you are convinced you want to stay, her pain will stop."

"How long do you plan on keeping us here?"

"It should not take long."

"To test me? To empower me?"

"Yes."

"Then where do we go?" Mark asked.

"Nowhere. You will strike from here."

"You're kidding, right?"

"No. This type of ability is not bound by space or time."

"You tell me more weird shit every time we talk. Are you saying I can kill your aliens from out here in the middle of nowhere?"

"You are not going to kill them. You are going to disable their main computer."

"Which computer is that?"

"It is a very sophisticated device. It monitors humanity. In a sense, it controls us. Once it is disabled, we will be free of this menace."

"They won't just fix it?"

Mr. Grimes was distant. "No. That would not be possible."

"Why not?"

He glanced at Mark. "You will see." He took a step toward the door Mark had exited. "May I help you with Jessa?"

Mark grabbed his arm. "Where is this alien computer?"

Mr. Grimes hesitated. "Near."

"How near?"

"It is closer than you can imagine."

8

The powers that be must have decided they were compatible, because they were given the same room. A nice place, with a Jacuzzi, a stocked refrigerator, wide views of the barbed wire fence and the desert beyond. The air inside the room was cool—the windows did not open; they were designed not to open. Two new faces carried Jessa inside and laid her on the bed. These guys were in their thirties, Italian perhaps, well built but with faces that did not smile. They exchanged perhaps four words with Mark. He was anxious to be rid of them, to be alone with Jessa. The move had awakened her. After the guys left, she looked around the room with wonder and pain.

"Are there condoms in the medicine cabinet?" she asked.

"I haven't checked. How are you feeling?"

"Swell. Does your Mr. Grimes want to share his tube of cream anytime soon?"

"I'm afraid not." He touched her bandaged leg lightly. "Is there anything I can do for you?"

"How about a cigarette?"

"You know I don't smoke."

She smiled. "Really? I thought you did."

"No. You shouldn't either, now."

"How far are we from Vegas?"

"Two hours. Why?" he asked.

"Let's escape to there tonight and you can marry me."

He had to smile. "You don't really mean that."

"I do mean it. But you never would."

"Why do you use that word—*never?*"

She lost her smile. "Because it is the one word that best describes my life."

He couldn't get her to elaborate.

They came for him that evening, Mr. Grimes and Dr. Brain. The latter was not merely fat but obese—hippo chin, no neck. Almost entirely bald, he combed his few remaining reddish brown hairs over the massive crown of his head. He wore white, like a doctor, and panted heavily between words. His eyes were a gentle blue, warmer than Mr. Grimes's. He had the aura of a doctor about him.

Mr. Grimes cut Dr. Brain's examination of Jessa short, an act Mark did not appreciate. Jessa was out of Percocet, and she needed more pills, or preferably something a little stronger. Mark let his feelings be known. Mr. Grimes raised a hand and spoke calmly.

"Then it is best we get to work immediately," he said.

"No," Mark corrected. "It would be best if you would let Jessa have more of the cream."

"You know the rules, Mark," Mr. Grimes said. "We cannot change them to accommodate you or Jessa."

"Because the people above you say so?" Mark asked.

"Yes," Mr. Grimes said.

"I am beginning to doubt these people exist," Mark muttered.

Dr. Brain cleared his throat. "We are sympathetic to both your positions. All we ask is that you trust us for a few days, and then you will see that what we tell you is the truth."

Mark had to try not to snigger. "So you believe in these aliens as well?"

"Yes," Dr. Brain said.

"Where are they? How did they invade Earth?"

"They came to Earth in huge star ships," Dr. Brain said. "We know that much. Their vessels are large enough to contain the entire population of Earth."

"Are you saying they mean to remove us all from Earth?" Mark asked.

Mr. Grimes spoke hastily. "They have that capacity, certainly."

Mark felt frustrated. "But you say the government doesn't even know that they're here. Why can't our scientists see these spaceships if they're so big?"

"They were cleverly cloaked," Dr. Brain said.

"Were?" Mark asked.

Mr. Grimes spoke. "I have promised that you will see the aliens before we require you to use your gift. It is better we concentrate on the latter and move forward." He added, "We don't have a lot of time."

"Why is the clock ticking?" Mark asked.

"We will leave that answer to your imagination." Mr. Grimes stood. "We are going to move now to a testing room, six floors below. It's heavily shielded and is impossible to eavesdrop on." He glanced at Jessa, who was stretched out on the bed, looking the worse for wear. "You will accompany us."

"No!" Mark protested. "She's injured. She's not part of these experiments. Why should she go with us?"

"Who said she's not a part of these experiments?" Dr. Brain asked gently, and he stared at her as he spoke. Jessa, who had been sitting unusually still, did not flinch at the question. She touched Mark's arm.

"It's all right," she said. "I want to go."

"But how can you move?" Mark asked.

Mr. Grimes snapped his fingers. The two bull-necked men from earlier in the day opened the door, a wheelchair nearby. "We are well equipped in this facility," Mr. Grimes said.

Jessa was gently lifted into the wheelchair by the two goons. Mr. Grimes wheeled her toward an elevator that was high-tech stainless steel and large enough to accommodate all of them. The two guys remained on top, perhaps for reasons of security. The elevator hummed as it descended—Mark received the impression that they were going down more than six stories. There were twenty buttons on the elevator control panel, none of them numbered.

The testing room was large and oval, dominated by a long wooden table that echoed the contours of the room. Around it were spaced twenty comfortable chairs, each securely bolted to the floor. The ceiling and carpet were warm yellow, the lights recessed. Mark found the room both relaxing and intimidating. The design was benign, but he was aware of the past tensions in the room, probably from experiments that had been performed on others. He wondered where those others were now.

Mr. Grimes gestured for him to have a seat at one end. Jessa remained nearby in her wheelchair. In the center of the table, in a large metal dish, was a wadded-up newspaper. Mark noted video cameras on either side of the room. They moved as he moved, perhaps his tests would be examined later by others. Mark now did believe that Mr. Grimes and Dr. Brain had people—and money—behind them.

"Can you guess what we want you to do now?" Mr. Grimes asked when they were all seated. He appeared a tad nervous; maybe he feared Mark would set him and Dr. Brain on fire.

"Make the newspaper catch fire with my mind," Mark said, bored.

"Exactly," Mr. Grimes replied.

"And how am I supposed to do that?" Mark asked.

"It will help if you close your eyes and breathe deeply for a few minutes," Dr. Brain suggested. "You may both do this, do it now."

"This is crazy," Mark mumbled as he complied nevertheless. He could hear Jessa breathing beside him. Yet the breathing did help, and he found himself relaxing. Dr. Brain spoke in a soothing tone.

"Keep your eyes closed, it is not necessary to open them again during the experiment. It is enough that you know what you wish to burn, where it is, and what it is. The distance and size of your target do not matter because your ability is not bound by such matters. Even time does not matter in the mind. But not believing in yourself, in your ability, can affect you. For that reason, we ask that you try to drop your doubts. Only for now—when the experiment is complete, you may again question what is true and what is false.

Continue to breathe easily and deeply. Feel every muscle in your body relax. Where there is tension, let your mind go to that spot and feel that tension dissolve."

Dr. Brain had a hypnotist's voice. Almost despite himself, Mark began to relax deeply. His breathing slowed involuntarily as his mind came to focus on the doctor's suggestions. He knew that the man was in a sense hypnotizing him, but because he still felt in control, he didn't mind. Dr. Brain was silent for several minutes, then continued in an even softer tone; he was no longer panting between words.

"Now I want you to imagine a point of focus between your eyebrows. A point where all the powers and resources of your mind gather effortlessly. Simply be at this point of focus. Bring your entire attention there. It is a place well known to the ancient mystics. Some call it the spiritual eye, others call it the doorway to God. It doesn't matter, for you it is a place of all possibilities. A place where your deepest abilities manifest. You don't have to try to burn the newspaper. You simply want to, and because you want to, it will burn. But do not feel rushed. There is no hurry to complete the experiment. Do not worry whether you succeed or fail. It doesn't matter because nothing matters at this point of focus. You are happy there, free, you feel as if you have stepped through a doorway into a greater reality."

Dr. Brain fell silent for an unknown period of time. The weird thing was, Mark did feel free. He was aware of the room still, the people present, but neither dominated his awareness. It was as if space mattered more, the wide realm he suddenly found himself floating in. The area between his eyebrows pulsed. He discovered that if he focused on it, the feeling of expansion would increase. He found the process pleasantly paradoxical—he was intensely concentrating but was not using any effort. From deep inside he framed the simple wish: the newspaper should burn. He didn't care if it did or didn't. The room was a faraway place. Even Jessa was only someone he knew from another life.

More time elapsed. Floating, peacefully floating.

He became aware of a monitor nearby.

The electronic beeping of his heart.

The soft hiss of a ventilator.

He thought the word: *MAZE*.

It was not the name of a chemical.

It was the answer. To all.

Only he did not know the question.

He heard a sound. A repressed exclamation of pleasure. He smelled smoke, felt a faint wave of heat brush his brow. The two men shifted in their seats. Mark did not know all the rules of the experiment. He doubted he would have followed them even if he knew. Without waiting for further instruction, he opened his eyes.

The newspaper was on fire.

"Cool," Jessa said next to him, and she smiled. Yet he noticed the strain on her face. Dr. Brain's soothing voice had not worked its hypnotic miracle on her. Dr. Brain and Mr. Grimes were almost congratulating themselves. They had not been as convinced of his ability as they had professed. He noted the relief in their expressions, the hints of awe.

"You have done well, Mark," Mr. Grimes said with feeling. "On your first try—we are impressed."

Mark continued to feel power in his head.

"This will be my last try if you do not give Jessa the cream now," he said.

The newspaper continued to burn. Smoke did not accumulate in the room. From the ceiling Mark heard the whirr of an invisible fan. The facility was indeed well equipped. Yet the two men did not know how to deal with him. He had meant what he said, and they understood he was not bluffing. He was puzzled that *he* was not more impressed with the burning paper. Yet a part of him had known the experiment would go exactly as it had. As if he had already done it ahead of time. He felt strangely separated from time right then because he had not come all the way out of his trance. He couldn't get the memory of the heart monitor out of his head. It had been so distinct, as if it had been set up right next to him. Jessa stroked his arm lovingly.

"I knew you could do it," she said.

He stared at her. "Did you know that the night I stepped into your dressing room?"

His question startled her. "I don't understand."

"After your final performance of *Season of the Witch?* Did you know?"

Jessa barely shook her head.

Mark surveyed the room and then spoke with authority. The brief experiment had lifted a veil from across his mind. He did not know what the beeping sound had meant, but he did understand that love was never that easy.

"I understand it now, part of the puzzle," he said.

"What part?" Mr. Grimes asked, and he was curious.

Mark nodded to Jessa. "You three are working together. You have been since the beginning."

Jessa gasped. She could not answer.

It broke Mark's heart that he was right.

9

He lay on the bed beside her but did not touch her. There was no clock in the dark room; it was late. He refused to speak to her after the experiment, but he had not fled from her, which said more than words could. The truth was he did still love her, but he had to wonder if she ever cared about him at all.

He felt her stir. She was awake. Her leg hurt no more because they used the magic cream, which they had always intended to use. Agreements made in secret before Mark came on the scene. They had merely been using her pain—*she* had been using it—to manipulate him. That hurt the worst, that he had been such a sucker.

She rolled onto her back and he saw her eyelashes blink in the faint light. She wore an oversize

T-shirt, nothing more. He imagined her bare legs cool against the soft sheets. She smelled nice, and he hated himself for wanting to kiss her. *They* knew how lonely he'd been. He wondered what other weaknesses they would exploit. He was sure they had a whole list of them.

"Do you want to talk?" she whispered.

"No."

"Should I leave?"

"Yes."

Injured voice. "Do you want me to leave?"

"No."

"Mark, we have to talk."

"No, Jessa, we don't. It won't help. You lied to me. You have been lying to me all along. If we talk, you'll lie to me some more. I don't think I could bear that, not now."

She was silent for a while. "How did you figure it out?"

He sighed. "I don't know. I guess a part of me knew all along. You were the new girl on campus: sexy, talented, pretty. No one knew where you were from, but all the guys wanted you. I stumbled into your dressing room and overnight you fell in love with me." He shrugged. "Things like that don't happen in the real world. Not to guys like me they don't."

She reached out to touch him, thought better of it. There was a lamppost outside their window. In the glow he saw the devastation on her face, talented actress that she was. She shook her head against the pillow.

"You have no idea how wrong you are," she said.

"Because I have no idea how much you really love me? Yeah, I heard that one before. The least you can do is treat me like I have a brain. Dr. Brain does—and where the hell did that guy get that name anyway? No, don't answer that, I don't care. I don't care about anything anymore. You came to our school for one purpose—to get me out here in this desert with these weird guys who think the world has been invaded by aliens."

"But the world has been invaded by aliens."

He turned away. "You're the goddamn alien, Jessa."

She put a hand on his shoulder. If he had been half a man he would have brushed her hand away and told her to go to hell. He would have gotten up and dressed and left the compound that night, assuming they didn't shoot him in the process. He was all talk, a tool to be used and discarded. Perhaps Jessa was as well, but somehow he didn't think so.

"You don't understand," she said.

"I don't want to," he mumbled.

"I know you still care about me."

"That's my problem. I'll get over it."

"Please turn around and talk to me," she pleaded.

"No."

"What are you going to do then?"

"Try to sleep. In the morning I'll eat a good breakfast and try to leave here. Maybe the aliens will give me a ride to Vegas."

"You can't leave here," she said.

There was a frightening note in her voice.

He rolled back over and faced her. "They'll stop me?"

She watched him. "You will be stopped."

"By whom?"

"I can't say."

"Why not?" he demanded.

"You're not ready for the truth."

"Thanks for deciding that for me. I was worried I might have to decide for myself."

"You told me not to lie to you."

"No. I told you that you would lie to me. In fact, I think you're lying right now." He stopped. "What does MAZE mean?"

Her expression grew intense. "Why do you bring that up now?"

He frowned. "I'm not sure. Answer my question. And don't give me the long name of some stupid drug I can't pronounce."

"But you took the drug, you know it."

"Why did you give it to me? It wasn't because of my mother."

"I needed to open you up," she said.

"For what?"

"For what is to come." She paused. "The experiment today was nothing. Tomorrow the others will gather. They're like you and me—they have special abilities. They've been waiting for you because you are the key."

"What is your special ability?"

"I'm good in bed." She forced a smile. "Of course you don't remember."

"Did we really have sex?"

"Yes."

"How was I?" he asked.

"Incredible."

He groaned. "Maybe I believe that. Anyway, what is your special ability?"

She sat up in bed and stared out the window. In the dim light her face was lovely, that of an ancient statue, tomorrow's mystery. It was odd how he could contemplate his difficulties with her while Earth was supposedly overrun with aliens. He didn't know if his priorities were messed up or he was the only one in the whole compound who wasn't insane.

"I can remote view," she said. "Do you know what that is?"

"Yes. The military used it back in the eighties and nineties as a means of gathering intelligence data, but discarded the technique as unreliable. So you're able to project a portion of your consciousness outside your body and view a remote location?" He paused while she nodded. "Are you that good at it?"

Her gaze remained outside the window. "I'm so good that I can take others with me," she said.

"I didn't know that was possible."

She looked at him. "There are a lot of things you can't imagine."

He sat up as well. "I suppose you take the *others* with you when you remote view?"

"Yes."

"Is that how you were able to spy on the aliens?"

"Yes."

"I hope you have proof of their existence other than that supplied by your remote viewing."

"Why do you say that?"

"Because that kind of proof is all in the head, and nothing you see while remote viewing can be taken as hard fact."

"What about your ability to start fires? Is that a hard fact?"

Mark was evasive. "My eyes were closed during the experiment."

"Grimes and Brain did not set that newspaper on fire. You did it with your mind. Accept it and get over it." She rubbed her head as if it ached. "There is a lot of weird shit going on these days."

"Is that how you found me? Through remote viewing?"

"No. Grimes told you the truth. His people have had you under observation for a long time. You inherited your ability from your father, which he got from his father. The trait is passed down on the male side."

"But they sent you to my school to hook me?"

"Yes." She took his hand. "But that doesn't mean that I am incapable of caring for you."

His voice was bitter. "But even if you didn't care for me, you had to act like you did?"

"You can't think of that. It's not the way it worked out."

"Did they want you to give me MAZE?"

"No, that was from me." She paused. "Maybe it was a mistake."

"Why? It didn't have any lasting effect on me."

She studied him. "Don't you wish sometimes that you could run away and leave your life behind?"

Her question was not casual. Perhaps that was why it disturbed him so. Yet he didn't understand why he felt a stab of panic as she spoke. Once again, it was almost as if he knew she would ask the question. As if they had already had this conversation, which was finished by his yelling at her, and telling her he'd never see her again. The feeling was light-years beyond déjà vu. The MAZE chemical could still have been active in his brain. Between heartbeats, he heard the monitor beep again. It sounded so near when she leaned forward to study him closer. Perhaps she had repeated her question, to torture him—he was having trouble hearing. He didn't want to answer it. He was sure she knew his answer.

"No," he said with effort.

She persisted. "But it's what we all want. To escape to a far-off place where no one knows our names. You're no different from the rest of us."

"Wherever you are, you're still you. If you have problems, you take them with you."

She didn't like his response. "So you think there's no difference between heaven and hell? A saint would be happy in either place? A sinner would be miserable?"

"I wouldn't choose that example, but, yes, I guess. Why do you ask?"

She shook her head. "It doesn't matter. Tomorrow you'll see the aliens. You'll know they're real. Then you can decide if you want to help us."

"Grimes spoke of a central computer. That if it could be disabled, the threat of the aliens would pass. Have you seen this computer?"

"Yes."

"What does it do?"

"It monitors us."

"All of us?" he asked.

"In a general fashion. It doesn't study particulars. It observes and evaluates the society as a whole."

"For what purpose?" he asked.

She lowered her voice. "To see what we would have made of ourselves."

"Why do you use past tense?"

She shrugged. "It was a slip."

"Dr. Brain used past tense when he spoke of the alien ships. Was that a slip?"

"You focus on the strangest things," she said.

"I do not feel that is strange. When did this invasion occur?"

She hesitated. "Ten years ago."

He gasped. *What?*

"I know it's hard to accept, but it is true. It happened at the turn of the century. For a whole decade we have not been our own masters."

"But life goes on as it has always gone on. What kind of control are these aliens exerting?"

"Total control. We are puppets to them."

"Yet you said that they observe and evaluate us. That sounds like they don't interfere. You can't have it both ways."

A grim chuckle. "You will see."

"How will I see? You'll take me somewhere via remote viewing?"

She nodded. "Tomorrow. Grimes and Brain had planned a whole sequence of experiments to give you confidence in your burning ability, but you don't need it. You can melt steel as easily as light paper on fire. It is all a question of focus.

They have decided you will meet the others to-morrow and, with my help, project into the aliens' stronghold."

"Where is it located?" he asked.

"I can't tell you."

"Do you know?"

"Yes." She paused. "The truth is staggering. If I tell you, you'll freak out."

"I already am freaked out. Tell me."

"No. Trust me on this. You have to see for yourself."

"But I won't be seeing for myself. I'll be seeing through your eyes."

"No. I'll only be your channel to view them. You'll see what's there and you'll accept it as real because it is real." She lowered her head and stroked his arm. "I have lost your trust, haven't I?"

"To put it mildly. You know what really gets me? How I suffered about your burn. Had I been able, I would have taken the pain on myself." He shook his head. "I'm such an idiot."

She looked up. "No. You're extraordinary. I know you meant what you said. You care so much that you would rather suffer than have someone else suffer."

He snorted. "Me? You forget I'm the guy who started the fire that killed a few hundred peo-ple."

She pressed his hand to her chest. "That wasn't you, Mark. That was a setup."

He felt cold all over. "What do you mean it was a setup? I decided to do it." He stopped. "I did decide, didn't I?"

She wouldn't look at him. "Nothing is as it seems. We're all lost, have been for two—for ten years."

The cold remained. "Since the aliens came?"

"Yes," she said.

He began to boil inside.

She lied and told the truth at the same time.

Two years? Ten? How many really?

"It's like we're caught in a maze?" he asked.

She did look at him. "That's it, exactly."

A clue, he sensed it. "Where are the aliens?"

"Close."

"Where?" he insisted.

"Very close."

"And they look human?"

"Yes."

"Just like you and me?"

"Yes."

"Exactly?"

"Mark . . ."

He yelled. "Who are they?"

"No! You have to wait and—"

He shook her. *Who are you?*

She stared at him in shock as they both realized

he had his fingers around her throat. Slowly he let go of her. So many things he didn't understand, not least of which was his love for her. More than anything in their demon-haunted world, he wanted to make love to her.

Touching her neck gingerly, she sighed and wiped at her eyes. Tears in the night, threats in the dark, horror for breakfast. Mark didn't want to see the aliens—he didn't want them to be real. He had a terrible thought—if he had continued to choke her the nightmare would have ended. Even his mother would come back. But he could not destroy that which he loved, and he feared that was how he was to be destroyed. She was his witch, a devil disguised as an angel. Hell would be their next remote-view destination, and she would convince him it wasn't so bad.

Merely another place to run away to.

MAZE. She would not answer his questions about it.

She wept quietly. "I'm so sorry."

He brushed her damp cheek. "I'm the one who should apologize." He had to force the next word because he realized she might have lied about her name as well. "Jessa."

She grasped his hand and kissed it hungrily. "I love you, I do. I know you don't believe me, but if you give me half a chance I will prove it to you, Mark, I swear it."

He cupped her chin with his hand and lifted her head. He came close to kissing her, but instead spoke in a voice that was more than a whisper, but less than a vow.

"Don't lie to me again," he said.

"I won't," she promised.

10

The next morning, after breakfast in their room—cornflakes, milk, and orange juice for Mark, strawberry yogurt and a banana muffin for Jessa—they sat in the testing room with three other young people. Two were twentyish females, one blond and plain, English perhaps, the other coal black, an exotic beauty from God knew where. The guy was perhaps twelve years old, Japanese, with dark eyes that seldom blinked. All three wore black unisex uniforms. None seemed talkative, although each nodded to Mark. Jessa didn't say two words to the others, but it was obvious she had seen them before. They all sat waiting.

Mr. Grimes and Dr. Brain appeared. The former was his usual cool self, but the good doctor appeared nervous. They both asked how Mark had slept. He didn't know what to say. He hadn't made love to Jessa, although she had desperately wanted him to. He had refused out of principle, but perhaps if he had been less high-minded he might have slept and not just dozed. He had a lot on his mind, to state it mildly: aliens were all around and his girlfriend was weird.

"Is there anything we can get you?" Mr. Grimes asked Mark. It disturbed Mark that Grimes ignored the others.

"Painkillers," Mark said.

"Are you in pain?" Dr. Brain asked, concerned.

"No. But in this place I'm worried that I will be."

Mr. Grimes ignored the comment. "This process is entirely safe. We have tested it numerous times. As I explained, the aliens are unaware of human psychic abilities. They cannot even imagine they exist. Using remote viewing—with the help of the group—you will enter their stronghold and move about undetected."

Mark gestured. "Will we all be together?"

"Yes," Mr. Grimes said.

"But you may not be able to see us," Jessa said. "Not the first time. It takes practice."

"Am I to burn anything while I'm out and about?" Mark asked.

"No," Dr. Brain said quickly, and glanced at Mr. Grimes, who clamped back a response. Clearly Grimes wanted Mark to strike while the iron was hot, so to speak. Dr. Brain added, "This is an exercise."

"What are the special abilities of the others in the room?" Mark asked. He wanted the others to reply, but Grimes was the boss.

"That information is not important at this time," he said.

"To you," Mark corrected.

"We simply want you to become familiar with moving around in this manner," Dr. Brain said. "You understand remote viewing is not a true out-of-body experience. You are only projecting a portion of your mind—that is all. Another part of you will still be here in this room. You may even still be aware of this room, it won't matter."

Mark nodded. "I understand."

"Good," Mr. Grimes said as he took a seat beside Dr. Brain at the far end of the table, away from the others. Today there was no metal dish with a newspaper to burn. The long wooden table was bare. Mr. Grimes nodded to the black beauty—apparently she was to be the hypnotist today. She glanced at Mark before telling them all to close their eyes; Mark did as he was told, but he wished he knew her name.

He had no expectations that he would see anything.

The young woman's voice was enchanting.

"Breathe in through your nose, out through

your mouth," she said. "Breathe at your own rhythm, but breathe slow and deep. The exhalation is naturally longer than the inhalation. Take in fresh revitalizing energy, exhale stale energy from your system. Relax into the breath, feel it is happening to you, not that you are making it happen. A greater force breathes through you, keeps you alive. Relax into that force, it is all around you."

Mark felt as if each breath expanded his lungs slightly. Relaxation stole over his body; he wished he had known this simple exercise years ago. Maybe he could have gotten his frustrations out this way, rather than burning stuff. The young woman's voice was delicious. He wondered if they had hired her for her voice alone. She continued in a softer tone.

"Now we settle into ourselves, into the space between our eyebrows. Feel the pulse there, the magnetism. Consciousness moves toward an effortless focus, a pleasant singularity. There may come light, there may be simple silence. Above all else feel yourself center there, at this doorway into another realm. Be still—do not push aside the thoughts, but do not encourage them, either."

Mark shifted into an expanded focus. Once again he found the state paradoxical—he was calm but highly attentive. The young woman continued to speak, but now he heard her words inside his head. It was as if an eye inside his skull were slowly opening. He saw images of burning stars and tumbling asteroids, of huge planets and whirling nebulae. They were faint but colorful, three-dimensional paintings from a cosmic master. They rushed by as if he traveled at an incredible velocity. A portion of him understood that the woman was suggesting they expand across the galaxy. Her instructions were subtle and spoke to his subconscious. There was power in her voice, there was no other way to explain what he was experiencing.

The rush into deep space did not continue forever. Far away he heard their guide order them to shrink inside, to penetrate the deeper layers of matter. Mark felt as if he had bumped into a single atom and dived inside it. He saw the vibration of the quantum level, spinning electrons that were both matter and energy simultaneously. His soul peered at the atom nucleus, and then suddenly he was flying through it, a supernova exploding before his internal vision, followed by a miniscule black hole drawing all existence back into itself. The blackness remained, an unimaginably vast abyss where nothing moved. He felt as if his own breathing had stopped and wondered if he was dead. The idea did not disturb him.

Indeed, it resonated with profound truth.

His inner eye opened all the way.

He was standing on a metal grid that stretched away from him for what appeared to be miles. Above and below were other such grids, permanent scaffolds that ran along huge glass tanks filled with blue liquid. The metal grid was without a railing. Those who walked it with physical bodies possessed steady nerves. The tanks were on his right; to his left was a drop down to what appeared to be a massive generator, which was not enclosed. It burned with the brilliance of a violet sun. He assumed the energy generated was channeled by powerful magnetic fields. There was no question that he was witnessing technology centuries beyond what mankind had developed.

Above was only blackness, which made him feel he was far underground. He moved along the metal grid as it bent around the transparent blue tank. Dark objects bobbed inside the liquid, but he didn't stop to examine them. Sparks flared in the depths of the tank. He heard voices ahead, soft-spoken beings discussing technical facts. He wanted to see if these people were aliens because he remembered just then where he was supposed to be. The place was not as he had imagined it would be.

He came upon two individuals, a man and a woman. They appeared to be of Nordic or Germanic descent, fit and muscular, mid-twenties. Even in the violet light cast by the generator below, he could see they both had blond hair and blue eyes. Their dress was unisex bodysuits, gray with black borders. Each wore a silver badge over the heart—a device of some kind, perhaps for communicating. Their hands flickered over a lit control board as they spoke, oblivious to the fact that they were being observed. Mark thought they were two of the most beautiful creatures he had ever seen.

Their words were foreign to him, but it was clear that the two were helping to maintain whatever it was that floated in the blue tank. Again Mark gazed around and felt awe at the size of the underground chamber. There were tanks as far as he could see, but only these two people. He wondered where the central computer was.

His thought had strength. No sooner had he thought the question than he found himself being whisked away from the couple and deposited at the base of the generator. The glowing machine was encircled with an elaborate hive of fiber-optic strands. The complex mass was a rainbow of technology, but Mark saw no obvious way to control the generator, no buttons or knobs. Nevertheless, he knew he was looking at the central computer of which Mr. Grimes and Jessa had spoken. The device that was supposed to monitor all of humanity.

But where was he exactly?

Where was humanity in relationship to this computer?

A disquieting sensation one step removed from total recognition dawned. He looked up at the endless rows of metal catwalks crisscrossing high above him. He could not see the handsome couple but knew they were up there somewhere. At the moment he didn't care about them, nor about the computer. The dark objects floating inside the blue tanks—he had to see what they were. Anxiety swept over him because the mystery was about to be solved. What he would see could explain everything.

Now he was not sure he wanted to know.

Mark found himself back up on a metal grid. Alone.

He peered into a tank as a dark shape bobbed by. It appeared as large as a cantaloupe and was gray, pink, and jellylike. There were valleys and canals carved upon its surface. Mark realized in horror that it had taken a lifetime to make it. Decades of life and experience, of love and pain, of innocent days spent beneath a warm sun. All to end up here, cruelly severed, forsaken in an alien storage tank filled with electrically charged blue fluid. Observed and categorized, dissected and judged.

His nightmarish vision on MAZE.

Mark understood that he was looking at a human brain.

Billions of them harvested and placed in these tanks.

Still living, sort of. At least still believing that life existed.

The aliens had not merely conquered Earth.

They had consumed humanity.

He knew he stared at his own brain.

11

Once more, in darkness, Mark lay beside Jessa. Neither slept; Mark was afraid to close his eyes. It was late but it was hard to acknowledge the lateness. Time had never been so relative. Dream time dominated; he prayed for the painful jar of an alarm. Where were the aliens? Only a few feet from the test tube. Mark's pajamas could not smother the chill that radiated from his chest. He had never felt so naked. An ironic thought for someone who no longer possessed a body.

He had been unable to talk to the others all day.

He had wandered alone in the desert. They had let him.

Jessa touched his arm. He found that ironic as well, her having fingers. He tried not to think about what she really looked like, but it was all he could think about. Life was a sham, the whole world nothing but sparks dancing between currents of blue slime. He wanted to vomit, but he'd done that already and there was nothing left in his stomach. He did not like Jessa touching him. It gave him the creeps.

"Mark," she said.

"Yes?"

"Can we talk about it?"

"No."

"We have to talk about it."

"No."

She got up on her elbow. "I told you the truth would freak you out."

"That was an understatement."

"Are you mad at me?"

"No. I don't think I'll be able to experience 'mad' again—or any human emotion for that matter. I'm in shock, yes, that is what I am and all I am." He shook off her hand. "Do you mind not talking to me?"

She was in obvious pain. "All we have is each other."

He stared at the ceiling. "It's not possible for us to have each other."

"You have to shake this off. I had to do it, the others as well. There are things we have to do, plans we must make."

"I don't think so."

"Are you just going to give up?" she asked.

MAGIC FIRE

"I would say that would be a reasonable thing to do at a time like this. We have been gathered and gutted. The show is long over as far as I can tell."

"You don't even know where we are," she said.

"I do. In the blue tanks." He drew in a ragged breath. "I wish they would let us drown. But I suppose that's no longer possible."

"We are in the blue tanks, but we're no longer on Earth. We're no longer even in our century."

He felt a stir of curiosity and resented it. "What do you mean?"

She sighed and stared out the window. "The alien vessels came for us at the turn of the century—the doomsayers were right. But none of them foresaw an Armageddon like this. We have studied the aliens' thoughts and have some idea of what happened. The human race was knocked unconscious from outer space—some type of high-intensity energy burst. Then the vessels descended, collected us, and harvested our brains." She trembled. "Our brains were separated from our bodies and frozen. Even though this alien race has extraordinary technology, they've been unable to crack the light barrier. We suspect it cannot be broken, that the speed of light is the fastest any object can travel in this galaxy. The aliens travel between stars in a state of suspended animation. We traveled with them back to their home world in the same state.

141

The only difference is that they left our bodies behind."

"Bummer," Mark muttered. He had thought they were still on Earth, beneath the surface, but he supposed it didn't matter. Nothing did.

"As Mr. Grimes told you, their home world is four hundred and twenty light-years from Earth. It took over four centuries for us to get here. It is now at least the twenty-fifth century—we're not sure but we think the aliens took another century before they thawed out our brains and reactivated our minds. For us it seemed like the next day. The last ten years of our lives have not happened. They have been mere projections of what we think would have happened in our world. These projections are important to the aliens. They must be or they wouldn't have gone to so much trouble to preserve our brains. I told you, their computers monitor us closely."

Despite himself, Mark found her remarks fascinating.

"Do you know why they did this to us?" he asked.

Jessa nodded grimly. "It appears the reason we look like them is that they planted human life on Earth. They have been observing us for thousands of years. We suspect they have carried out similar experiments on many worlds. That is what humanity is to them—an experiment. Then, when we reached a certain level of development, they harvested us. Grimes thinks that our ventures into space triggered their invasion, but he's not sure. Certainly we were no threat to them, and would not have been for centuries to come."

"But why do they let us go on thinking we're alive?"

"They want to see what we would have done as a race."

"But if they had left us alone, they could have observed the same thing. With a lot less trouble."

Jessa shook her head. "Now they have total control over the experiment. They can alter it as they please. They can stop it whenever they want."

Mark had not thought of that possibility. "Are they altering our supposedly normal development?" he asked.

"We're not sure. Grimes is not even sure if our attempts to get back at them have not been inspired by them."

Mark frowned. "But they control everything. How could they not know what we're doing?"

"We're operating on the assumption that they are monitoring the *general* direction of our imagined development. As you were told, they appear to have no understanding of psychic abilities. Perhaps such abilities have never shown up in their other experiments. It's possible that their computer is not programmed to take note of such activities. Grimes says that you cannot look for what you cannot imagine."

Mark was not convinced. "They're probably recording our words as we speak."

"It's possible. Do you want to focus on that possibility? It leads to despair."

"You don't have to lead me anywhere. I'm already there."

She was annoyed. "So you're quitting on us?"

"I am already choking on the sidelines. Remember, I don't have a body anymore. You don't, either." He glanced at her body and added with disgust, "I hate this."

"I'm still me, Mark."

He turned away. "No, you're not."

She spoke to his back. "I gross you out? Is that it?"

"Yes. Sorry. I'm old-fashioned, I like my girls with their brains attached to their bodies."

"You have to help us."

"No. I don't have to do anything. It's all being done for us."

"That's not true. We have lost our bodies, but we haven't lost our humanity. We can still beat them."

"Really? I'd say they sort of have the upper hand at this point."

She grabbed him by the shoulder and rolled him back over. "You are our weapon. They have no defense against you. We need you to project outside your body once more and set their goddamn computer on fire. That will short out the tanks and short out this illusion. Humanity will be set free."

He had not understood what they were driving at.

"Humanity will not be free," he said quietly. "Humanity will die."

She swallowed. "It has to be done. We were never meant to live in a cage."

Mark sat up. "You mean you guys are going through all this just to commit suicide? Is that what all this is about?"

She nodded tightly. "Yes."

"I don't believe it."

A note of agony entered her voice. "What is there to believe? What else is there to do?"

He shook his head. "You're lying."

She punched the bed. "I am not lying! Goddamn you for saying that!"

He grabbed her hands. "Shh. This is not you, Jessa. I know you."

She sobered. "I'm the one who always says that. Why are you saying it now?"

"Because you're a witch and you have magic. You have something up your sleeve you're not telling me. You always do."

She stared. "Even if I did, what do you care? You've already abandoned me."

He shrugged. "From where I sit the situation looks hopeless."

Jessa nodded tightly. "It is hopeless."

"Then why fight it?"

"It's hopeless for everyone except us two," she added.

He sat up. "What?"

She glanced around. "We're not being spied on."

"You don't look too sure of that," he said.

"I'm the one person in this whole compound who can be sure. You remember my special ability. Do you remember those two you saw while remote viewing?"

"You saw what I saw?" Mark asked.

"Yes. I was beside you the whole time. Those two are always at work around the tanks. These aliens seldom rest. They will be there days in a row. But they are the only ones who come into this place. The equipment is highly automated. Those two are the only ones needed to take care of five billion brains."

"And the computer," he added.

"The computer is not important, either, not to us. Listen to me! I have a plan. While outside my body I've bumped into that woman a few times. I have actually been inside her body, inside her mind. Each time I entered she became dizzy, but passed it off. But the truth is I know I can take over her body."

Mark was stunned. "You mean, permanently?"

146

"Yes! And if I can do it, you can do it as well."

"You want the two of us to share her body? Sounds kinky."

"No! You can shove the guy out of his body. You can do it, with my help."

"Wait a second. You're moving too fast. As Dr. Brain explained—now I know where he got his name—when we remote view we don't really leave our bodies—or our brains. We merely project a portion of our minds."

Jessa shook her head. "That's true, but the rest of the group doesn't know that. They can't imagine what I have stumbled onto."

"Why don't you share it with them?"

Jessa was anxious. "I can't."

"Why not?"

"Because I can't save them all. I can't find bodies for them all. Or if I tried, the alien society would become alert to what was happening and destroy us all."

"You don't know that for sure," Mark said.

"No, but it would probably happen. We would die, with the rest of humanity. But this way, the two of us can escape this nightmare."

"And set humanity free?"

The question stopped her. "Yes. Once we have taken possession of their bodies, you can destroy the main computer."

"What makes you so sure I can get inside this guy?"

"I'll put you inside him. My talent is highly developed. I have worked with Grimes for two years. Trust me."

He understood that he was contradicting himself from a minute ago, but he felt compelled to speak. "You say that often, Jessa. But this issue goes beyond trust. We are talking about mankind. They may all be trapped in a cage, but they don't know that. They have their lives, or they think they do. Five billion people—or brains—is not something we can wipe out because we *think* it's for the best."

Jessa was cool. "Your argument is highly moralistic. It is also bullshit. We cannot ask five billion people what they would do in this situation. We cannot make an announcement on the Internet and call for a vote. We have to move fast and decisively. We will not have a chance to take over the aliens twice. They will guess something is up and bring in help. Tomorrow morning, during the session, we have to strike." She paused. "It will be our last session."

"You honestly won't tell the others what you're up to?"

"No," she said firmly. "You cannot tell them, either."

"But they're your friends. There aren't many of them here at this compound. If you're as good as you think you are at pushing these aliens out of their bodies, then why don't you at least give it a shot with the whole gang?"

"I have told you why. It raises our chances of failure. Also, this alien couple is isolated here. We can work them over until we succeed. But up there . . ." Jessa glanced at the ceiling. "There are millions of them. There would be no control."

"Doesn't it bother you? Leaving the others behind?"

"No. Yes, of course. But all they hope for at this point is death. We can give them that. Why should I give them false hope beyond that?"

Mark found her arguments logical; nevertheless, her attitude stunned him. She spoke of the death of five billion so easily. He couldn't help but think of the death of his mother. Had she really died? Was her brain no longer functioning? Had it already been passed on for dissection? He understood that she had probably died—in the illusion—because she would have died in real life. Yet their dilemma raised many questions. His mother had been healthy as a horse ten years ago. Plus, what about all the babies that had supposedly been born in the last ten years? Were their brains alive?

Or were they only aliens?

He had lowered his head. She could see he was thinking and left him alone for a minute. But then she stroked his arm, kissed the side of his head, tried to hug him. He wanted to love her back, but somehow it didn't seem right.

"What is it?" she asked finally.

"I don't know," he said, and sighed. "Would I really have met you if none of this had happened?"

"Yes."

"You sound so certain."

She held his hands. "We are together because we are supposed to be together. It's not because we're trying to defeat the aliens. They have no part in us."

"That makes no sense."

She touched his hair. "But it's true, and you do have to trust me. That is why we have to escape together. Please, Mark, tell me that you will come with me."

He was pained. "We can't decide everything for the others. It's not right. Escape . . . escape . . ." He had trouble with the word, he did not understand why. He continued with difficulty. "Escape is not the solution. There is the world, there is life."

"There is no world!" she said sharply. "It is gone! The only chance for humanity lies with us two. You have to come with me—to refuse would be the act of a coward."

She had hit a bull's-eye. He knew he was not the coward, and it was wrong to do what she had planned. But he did love her, God forgive him, he couldn't help himself. It made him a partner in her sins. There was no argument he could use against her because she was the real key. It wasn't Grimes who commanded the compound. She had played all of them from the beginning and she would play them until the end. Even if she had to destroy a race in the process. He saw that about his beloved witch right then. No price was too high for her to pay.

"I will come with you," he said.

12

On the way to the session the next morning, Mark was stopped by Dr. Brain. The man wanted to speak to him in a private room, on the ground floor, close to the elevator. Mark had just had a light breakfast and was feeling distracted by what Jessa had planned. A part of him thought she wouldn't have the guts to go through with it. A larger part knew she was capable of anything.

"I'm in kind of a hurry," Mark said as he was led into what appeared to be Dr. Brain's office. The session was scheduled to start in five minutes, but Dr. Brain gestured for Mark to have a seat.

"This won't take long," the doctor said as he moved behind his desk chair. He didn't sit down, however. He appraised Mark briefly; there was no disguising his nervousness. He kept running a hand through his thin hair. His breathing was strained as he asked if Mark had slept well.

Mark settled in the chair. "Fine. What's this about?"

Still Dr. Brain did not sit down. "I want to talk to you about the session this morning. What you plan on doing during the remote viewing."

"I don't know what you guys have planned." Could the doctor have bugged their room? Jessa had assured him that she would have known. Dr. Brain cleared his throat as he gripped the back of his chair.

"Do you know why you are here?" he asked abruptly.

"Sure. To kill the aliens."

Dr. Brain showed a brief flash of anger, an odd expression on his usually pleasant face. He let go of the chair back and came partway around his desk. When he spoke next he tried to sound friendly.

"You are smarter than that, Mark," he said. "Yesterday you saw what the situation is. You know we are already beaten, defeated in the worst imaginable way."

"I admit it doesn't look good," Mark said.

Dr. Brain moved to his right. "You also must know that Mr. Grimes and I do not always agree on the direction this compound is heading. He wants to use you and the rest of the team as weapons. I'm sure you can now see there is no point in that."

"I didn't know there was such a fundamental

disagreement between you two," Mark replied. Dr. Brain circled behind him, giving Mark the creeps. He spoke to the back of Mark's head.

"I don't believe you, Mark. I watch your eyes, read your expressions. Besides being endowed with a powerful psychic ability, you are extremely intelligent."

That was the second time in ten seconds he had told him how smart he was.

"How do you want to use the team?" Mark asked.

Dr. Brain came around to Mark's right side and spoke passionately, his huge head a foot away. Mark smelled his perspiration, sensed his fear. Mark had been expecting this, after hearing Jessa. The compound could not be in complete agreement, not when mass suicide was the goal.

"As a bargaining chip!" Dr. Brain said. "We have something the aliens do not have. They will want it. They will give us a great deal to get it."

"Are you sure?" Mark asked. "They control us completely. What makes you think that once they become aware of what we're doing they won't just destroy us?"

Dr. Brain waved his arm. "That's Grimes talking. Has he talked to you?"

"Not about this, no."

Dr. Brain walked to the window and stared out. He continued to pant audibly, sounding as if he were on the verge of a heart attack. Mark wondered then how the doctor and Grimes had come up with the healing cream. He suspected one or both of them had gained a measure of control over the illusion. The cream was nothing—toothpaste—but the conviction that *everything* was nothing might give them the ability to manipulate their surroundings. Yet, Mark reminded himself, they needed him to burn the aliens, outside the illusion. His ability must be real in both realities.

Dr. Brain did not look like a master of anything. He acted like a desperate man. For the first time, Mark wondered if he was in danger.

"Grimes wants to kill us all, you know," Dr. Brain said quietly. "I'm sure Jessa told you the truth. True?"

Mark saw no point in lying. "Yes. But she agreed it was the only way out."

Dr. Brain whirled, his many pounds of flesh taking a second to catch up, the fat crisscrossing his midsection in waves.

"Jessa is full of schemes," he said angrily. "She acts like she agrees with Grimes when we all know she keeps her own counsel. What else did she talk to you about last night?"

"Nothing else comes to mind."

Dr. Brain stared at him intently. Then slowly he spoke, softening his voice. "Mark, do you want to die?" he asked.

"Not especially."

"Good. Let's return to my suggestion. I know for

a fact we can bargain with this race. Their technology is extraordinary. They cruise the galaxy, they plant and harvest entire races. I suspect they are millions of years ahead of humanity. Imagine what that means, what they could give us if they were pleased with us."

Mark shifted in his seat. Time was ticking. Dr. Brain seemed determined to keep him as long as it took. "What does it matter? They can't give us our bodies back."

Dr. Brain clenched his fists. "But they could give us back *some* kind of bodies! They could make them for us. I'm sure they could make whatever they wanted. Our brains could be transplanted into these bodies and we could live again. But follow Grimes's lead, destroy their central computer, and we perish as a race. I tell you it's insane. We have to stop him before it's too late."

"I'm confused," Mark said. "You've obviously worked for this guy for years. Why this sudden change of goals?"

"You! You were never here before. We could never end it before. Oh, we could spy on them all we wanted, but to what purpose? You are the crucial piece in the puzzle. You make Grimes's goal possible. Honestly, I never thought this day would come—not in this way." He stopped and spoke in a grim tone. "When we go downstairs, he's going to order you to destroy the computer."

"Are you sure?"

"He told me so last night."

"What did you tell him?" Mark asked.

"What I'm telling you now."

"What about the ancient order of mystics that directs Grimes. Do they exist?"

"He says they do. I have never met them myself. But the man has resources."

"Did he have these resources before the invasion?"

Dr. Brain was puzzled. "What are you asking?"

"How long have you known him?"

"Five years." Dr. Brain moved toward Mark again, impatient. "But who cares? All that matters is if you will help me or not."

Mark eyed the doctor, who stood close on his right.

"I have to think about it," Mark said.

"What is there to think about? You have the power to choose life or death. For everyone!"

"You know it's not that simple. We contact the aliens and try to bargain and if they don't like what they see, we might lose our only chance to stop this charade."

"They are advanced! They won't kill us out of fear!"

"We are descended from them," Mark said. "As a race, we often killed when we were afraid. They just have to throw a switch and all of us here at the compound are history. The situation has to be discussed with the group as a whole."

"The group will follow Grimes!"

Mark started to stand. "We'll see."

Dr. Brain stopped him with a heavy hand on his shoulder. He spoke in a low voice that was on the verge of cracking.

"You don't care about the group," he said. "You only care about making Jessa happy. I know her, I know how she uses people."

"Everybody in this compound is a user," Mark said, sitting very still. Out of the corner of his eye he saw the doctor grope in his pocket. Mark added, "You must know that the aliens would never make bodies for five billion people."

Dr. Brain kept his right hand in his white lab coat pocket, the other hand on Mark. Once more his voice changed. He sounded far way, speculating on places he knew in his heart he would never see.

"They needn't save everyone," he said. "A few would be all that matters. A handful is all it has ever taken to guide humanity. If a dozen of us survive, then mankind will go on. I will see to it." He paused, and his right hand flexed. "You're just a kid, and you don't understand. You can't be allowed to get in my way."

Mark brushed the hand off his shoulder and jerked out of the chair as Dr. Brain pulled a syringe from his pocket and stabbed at Mark's neck. Dr. Brain caught Mark's collar, nothing more, but didn't drop the needle. Mark backed quickly into the corner of the office. Dr. Brain now stood between him and the door. The fluid in the syringe was as clear as water, but Mark knew it was not so harmless. Dr. Brain indicated that he should stand still, a gesture Mark considered ridiculous. The doctor's eyes were glazed over with thoughts of his destiny. Mark suspected the guy dreamed of having his brain transplanted into one of those Nordic male bodies and being assigned to work with a team of beautiful blond aliens. Dr. Brain took a step toward him.

"You complicate the whole equation," he said. "You have to be eliminated."

"You won't get away with this," Mark swore.

"No? You can call out. They're all downstairs by now, so they won't hear you." He fingered the syringe. "It will be easier for you if you don't move. There will be less pain."

Mark's shoulder blades hit the corner. Dr. Brain had over a hundred pounds on him, not to mention the needle. Yet he was slow and out of shape. Still, Mark suspected the doctor only had to prick him with the needle to kill him. A doctor would know a thing or two about poisons. Mark would rush him only as a last resort.

Of course he was not completely defenseless.

His entire brain was supposed to be a weapon.

Mark narrowed his gaze, feeling power in his forehead. Dr. Brain felt it as well. He stopped dead in his tracks. The air seemed to shimmer with heat. Ozone cracked the carpet threads. Mark spoke with confidence.

"You're the one who taught me how to do this," he warned.

Dr. Brain shook his head. "You're scared. You can't concentrate."

"You look like the one who's scared to me."

Dr. Brain took another step. "You will die. We don't need you to bargain with the aliens."

Mark focused. The room temperature shot up ten degrees.

"Stop," Mark ordered.

Dr. Brain dripped sweat. Fear bulged his eyes out. "You can't do this! You're nothing! You're a goddamn teenager!"

"Put down the syringe. Now!"

Dr. Brain shuffled one step closer. He trembled violently. He was lucky not to drop the needle, or perhaps not lucky at all. Perspiration stains swelled the front of his white coat. He must have had a bad fever. Mark felt his forehead ache with pressure. Yet it felt good as well, better than sex.

"I'll kill you," Dr. Brain gasped, raising the syringe.

"Last warning," Mark whispered.

Dr. Brain lunged at him.

An invisible tongue leaped from Mark's forehead.

It happened as he thought of Dr. Brain's brain.

The doctor tripped hard and lay facedown on the floor, the top of his head inches from Mark's shoes. Mark rolled him over with his foot. Two narrow lines of blood ran down from the doctor's nose to his upper lip. His eyes stared straight up at the ceiling. He did not breathe. Mark suspected he had burnt out the man's neurons. Even though the guy had been trying to kill him, he still felt sick to his stomach.

Mark knelt and closed the doctor's eyes.

He picked up the undamaged syringe.

"Are you going to stab me with it?" a voice asked.

Mr. Grimes stood in the doorway. Mark didn't know how long he had been there and didn't really care. Grimes was dressed as always, immaculately in black—self-appointed undertaker for the human race. He glanced down at Dr. Brain, and if he felt sorrow over the death of his colleague, he didn't show it. His attention was mainly on Mark, the needle in his hand. It was odd, but the poison did tempt Mark. Yet he knew he would never do it, not to himself. He thought of Jessa then, with mixed feelings. Love and hate, the saying went, two sides of the same coin. Would she help him to escape, or was she still lying to him?

Of what use was the promise of a liar?

"Is he really dead?" Mark asked.

Mr. Grimes stepped into the room. "Do you mean can anyone die anymore? Or do they just think they're dead? To tell you the truth we aren't sure. Maybe their brains do perish in the alien tanks. Maybe they just sleep." He paused. "Are you asking about your mother or the doctor?"

The question annoyed Mark. That this demigod should presume to get personal with him. Yet the thought had come to Mark. That perhaps, somehow, he could speak to his mother again. At least pretend that he did. It was possible her brain floated alongside his in the blue liquid. He still felt her close, in his heart.

Only he didn't have a heart anymore.

"Did you know he would try to kill me?" Mark asked.

"Obviously not. I wouldn't have let him near you."

"But you knew he was unhappy with your plan."

Mr. Grimes raised an eyebrow. "Can anyone be happy anymore? What we do we do because we have to. We have no other choice."

"You expect me to burn out their computer this morning?"

"Yes. There is no reason to wait."

"What if I refuse?"

Mr. Grimes shrugged. "What can we do to you? Stick you with the needle?"

"You could."

Mr. Grimes looked weary. "Then maybe we will—I don't know. The team waits for us. What are you going to do?"

Mark looked down at the dead doctor.

"This is all bullshit," he muttered.

"It has been for ten years."

Mark looked up. "Should we leave him here?"

"Why not?"

Mark nodded. "Let's get this over with."

13

Mark was *outside*. The exotic young woman's voice worked as well as it had before. Listening to her speak in rhythm with the expanding cosmos, Mark doubted the sanity of what Jessa had planned. To kill these people because they could not bear the lie of their lives—and not to die with them—seemed a great sin. There had been no discussion before the session. Mark doubted the others knew that today was to be their last day. All of their eyes were closed and all of them were breathing deeply.

Mark moved inside. Subtler realms of matter.

He came to full awareness beside a transparent tank filled with blue fluid. He stood high on a metal catwalk. The violet power generator hummed far below. A brain swayed on the other side of the tank. It was as if it waved to him. He would have vomited if he'd had a stomach. Once again, he knew he was staring at what was left of his own body. He didn't understand how he could survive its destruction, even if he were inside the body of an alien.

A ghostly light flickered beside him. Jessa. She had told him to keep an eye out for her. He could see right through her, Casper flecked with miniature Christmas lights. But he couldn't see into her heart. He wondered how she'd betray him, in the end. By listening to her he was becoming like her. Her ghostlike presence gestured to the far side of the largest tank. Mark heard gentle voices—the tireless alien couple at work. He wondered how they felt about the brains they tended, if they wept when one floated to the surface and began to rot. They looked like nice people, only they and their kind had screwed humanity. Still, Mark felt bad for them.

Mark followed Jessa's ghost around the metal grid. It was odd but he couldn't see himself or any of the others on the team. Maybe they were off in secret alien alleys plotting their own escape. Perhaps Jessa did have the out-of-body control she had boasted of and could be dictating the exact movements of their adventure. There was something unnaturally powerful about her, something beyond her being a witch. He wondered if she had written the play she starred in at school. She had been such a natural to play the part. God, that night seemed a hundred years ago. Back then he had just wanted a girlfriend. Now look at him—Mr. Fire Brain himself, the fate of humanity held between his psychic-saturated synapses. He had not given Mr. Grimes the deadly syringe, it was still in his pocket.

MAZE. He thought of the drug.

He strained to hear the beep of the monitor.

Did the aliens monitor them with such equipment?

He saw no evidence of it.

They came upon the alien couple, whose language was foreign but musical to Mark. Jessa's ghost magically took on greater definition. He could still see through her, but the features of her face were now visible. The pinpoints of colored light inside her sparked and shifted as their hues darkened. She motioned for him to move in front of the male, who was standing five feet to the right of the female. He was a handsome creature. Mark wondered if he would feel pain and where his soul would go. Perhaps into the blue tanks? That would be fitting, but the prospect filled Mark with dread. Despite all evidence to the contrary, he could not be rid of the feeling that what they were doing was immoral.

In the vast cavern of tank after endless tank, he was suddenly possessed by the urge to find Dr. Brain's brain to see if it was OK. He hated the idea that his gift could only be used to hurt or destroy. It was hard not to think of his mother and her late-stage cancer agony, all part of a vast experiment. Yet the thought gave him a measure of bitter strength. When Jessa's ghost moved behind the man, and daggerlike ice spikes replaced her immaterial fingers, he didn't stop her. Perhaps there was galactic karma. He watched curiously as Jessa sank her astral daggers into the alien male.

The man flinched and dropped to his knees. The woman spun and rushed to his aid. Jessa's ghost reached a taloned claw into the man's heart region and yanked hard. Purple ectoplasm stained the air. The guy jerked like a puppet on a wire. He lost color and made a sick gurgling sound as he choked on his own saliva. Then he pitched forward into the woman's arms.

It was as if he were dead.

Mark felt himself being yanked forward, Jessa telling him to take a hint. He was pushed up against the guy's face even as the alien female rolled her partner onto his back and tried to resuscitate him. Mark didn't want to have his soul put in backward. He flipped over and settled into what seemed to be a corpse. He couldn't see the guy's spirit and didn't want to search for it. As he sank into the man's body, he heard a loud roar in what he assumed were the alien's ears. There was pain in his chest that felt oddly reassuring. He could feel and knew he must be alive—for the first time in ten years.

He coughed and opened his eyes.

The beautiful blond alien stared down at him anxiously.

"How are you feeling?" she asked.

He didn't get a chance to answer or even question how he could understand her. Abruptly a spasm shook her soft features and she fell on her side. Mark could no longer see Jessa but knew what she was up to. He sat up with effort, afraid to get in Jessa's way. The female did not vacate her body easily. She flayed on the metal grid, rolling precariously close to the edge. Her legs and arms thrashed and Mark could hear her speaking. He wondered what god she prayed to. What god would allow her and her kind to commit such heinous crimes against their own offspring.

Finally the female went still, and Mark waited in wonder. Was this possession or rebirth? How had Jessa known to do it? He feared what went through her mind when he wasn't watching. The young woman stirred and opened her eyes. Mark moved closer and helped her up. He felt a moment of intense anxiety. What if Jessa had failed and he was doomed to spend the rest of his life alone in this alien society?

But then she flashed a wicked smile and he knew his witch had won once again. She threw her arms around him and hugged him so tight he feared his ribs would be broken. It felt very natural to be held by her in their new bodies. The thought made him wonder, a tiny bit.

"I can't believe this," he gushed.

She sat back and beamed. "Piece of cake." She admired her hand and arms. "I think I'm stronger than I used to be."

"But not more lovely," he said.

She waved a hand as she stood. "You know you always preferred blondes to brunettes."

He hadn't known that and knew he'd never discussed the subject with Jessa. But he wasn't in the mood to argue.

There appeared no period of adjusting to his new body. It was as if he had been born alien. Jessa must have felt that way also because already she was leading him toward an elevator to take them down to the power generator. Mark could not help staring at the brains in the blue tanks, brains that looked so helpless and lost.

He stopped her at the elevator. "What language are we speaking?"

She paused. "Theirs. But we hear English."

"That's impossible."

"No. It's as it should be. We never think when we speak, we just speak. It's because our brains are wired for our language. These brains are wired for their language. Their ears as well. If you listen closely, you will see you are not really hearing English."

She was right, yet he did understand everything being said, and imagined it was English. He watched as she activated the control panel that operated the elevator.

"How do you know how to do that?" he asked.

"I just know." She gestured. "Do you understand the controls?"

He realized that he did. Everything the alien male knew, he now knew. His name was Lartza and his partner was called Dween. His was the better name he decided. Their official titles—inscribed on the electronic badges on their chests—resembled those of chief engineers. He outranked her, but only slightly. He was a Beta Class 6.9. She was a Beta Class 6.7.

They had their own apartment, which they shared with a daughter—Sharmti, six years old. XXY sector, Tower 1112, Floor 947, Room 98. Nice view of the spaceport, no noise from the silent silver ships—no pollution, either. Man, Mark thought, this was one amazing civilization. These people had colonized ten thousand solar systems and were capable of transforming the surface of any world. He marveled at their accomplishments with a curious sense of pride. The elevator door opened and Jessa pulled him inside. It was not much different from the one at the compound.

"We have to hurry," she said. "We have to destroy the central computer."

The elevator door closed and they started to descend.

"What's the rush?" he asked.

"Isn't it obvious?" she hissed. "The others will

realize what we've done. They'll try to do the same thing."

"Let them. We're out, and we're safe."

"No! We're not safe! I told you, if too many do what we've done, it'll attract attention. We can't risk it. Destroy the computer and the brains will die. Only then will we be safe."

Mark felt sick. They were almost down to the generator.

"I don't know if I can do it," he said.

"You have to do it!"

"No, I don't. You can do it, though."

She fretted. "I can't. The place is under constant observation. The authorities will have the equivalent of video tapes of what went on here today. The destruction must seem to have a supernatural cause. That way they'll never be able to figure out what went wrong."

"If I fry the computer, it might explode."

"It probably will. But I know the way out of here, and we'll be ready to run." She clasped his hands inside hers and spoke with feeling, her blue eyes bright. "I know I sound like a selfish bitch, but we have a deeper purpose here. Our race has been raped, and it is being raped daily. It must stop. If blowing up the computer kills us, we will still have to do it."

Mark was sad. "What will it be like for them? The whole world?"

The elevator halted and the door whooshed open. The violet light from the generator filled the small compartment. Jessa stood thoughtfully, pained even, but shook it off. She had that capacity to separate her feelings from reason: this feeling goes here, this moral is filed there—don't mix them up in case of implosion. She was simple and complex. Mystery needed paradox. They needed each other and neither knew why.

"They won't feel a thing," she said. "Everything will stop. The world will go black. It will be over."

He nodded past the lump in his throat. So the aliens felt emotion the same way. Aching hearts and salty tears. Curious they had not evolved beyond these primitive emotional reflexes. Perhaps he, Mark, imposed new sensations on the man's nervous system. He couldn't remember the alien crying. He dammed off the tears inside so Jessa couldn't see him acting so weak. He felt in conflict with every decision he had to make.

"It's not right," he mumbled.

She stared at him. "You'll be doing them a favor."

"And us?" he asked doubtfully.

Her eyes looked no different to him right then than they had the night she sat in front of her makeup mirror, scantily clad. She had invited him in and he dared hope he could ask her out. His heart pounded but she treated him well. That was all it took, he was a goner.

"We'll be all right," she, the actress, promised.

He knew that she lied. Always.

But he chose to believe her, it was less painful.

They approached the computer, which was actually one level below the glowing generator. The many strands of fiber optics—he remembered they were called Swing Squids—were more beautiful seen with physical eyes. Indeed, Mark was struck by how acute all his senses were. The aliens were the original humanoid models, stronger and more aware. Their computer was practically a living being. It knew they approached with a desire, and it wanted to be of assistance. Mark knew suddenly that he couldn't simply burn it out. The generator could explode in their faces. His alien memories explained this to him, and he explained it to Jessa.

"But we can't delay," she insisted.

Suddenly Mark felt the power in his head. His brain did not contain the psychic gift, his very soul must. The power continued to build between his eyebrows even though he was not yet focused. It was almost as if it were being pressed on him from the outside. Perhaps the collective consciousness of humanity begged him to stop its misery. Yet he struggled to push it aside; he didn't want to follow through with the horrific image that pressed into his mind. Jessa asked if he was in pain when he put a hand to his head. Maybe she feared the alien had come back for his body.

"No," he gasped. "Where is the way out?"

She pointed in the direction of a closed metal door behind them. "That leads to an elevator that will take us to the surface."

The magnetism in his head continued to build. He felt as if his brain would explode—when all the others did. No mere tongue of heat radiated from his forehead; it was more a shock wave from an atomic blast. He didn't want Jessa to get in the way of it. The blue fluid in the tank above them began to hiss with forming bubbles. This way was much more final. The liquid had begun to boil, the brains would disintegrate. Mark pushed her toward the door.

"Get out of here—it can't be stopped!" he yelled.

She stood, undecided. The invisible scorching wave swept to the right and left, down the long haunted cavern. Tank after tank began to bubble and hiss. Blue steam erupted through the vents at the top of the tanks. The silent sparks that were the foundation of humanity's decade-old illusion transformed into angry thunderbolts. Lightning struck the hard walls of the transparent containers. Cracks formed; scalding foam and dark brain matter poured onto the metal grids. Still, Mark felt the strength of the Magic Fire grow and spread, the wave of death that would not cease until all were safely dead.

He heard an unspoken sigh. It lifted his spirit

and broke his heart. Deep in the bowels of the vast cavern the roar of the shattering tanks almost deafened them. Yet the sigh remained and grew stronger. The nightmare truly was ending. Mark realized that what was happening was greater than he was. A higher power guided him. Had he simply shorted the computer, as Mr. Grimes had wished, it would not have been enough. Even if the generator had exploded, too many brains would have survived. The aliens could have continued with an abbreviated form of their experiment. This way it would be finished.

His part was over—the fire had a life of its own. They could leave now, not with clear consciences, but at least with the knowledge that it was out of their hands. Mark grabbed Jessa's arm and pulled her toward the exit. It meant a lot to him that she hadn't fled when the wave of flame had swept through him and the remains of humanity. Perhaps she really did love him. He knew that he loved her.

They had to hurdle a mound of burnt brains to reach the door. One last image of terror to take with them. Then they were in the elevator and going up. Jessa kissed him anxiously in the tiny compartment. She wouldn't let go of him. She kept saying how sorry she was. He didn't understand why. His tears came despite his strongest resolve.

Even the sight of the alien suns, yellow and red in a cerulean sky pulsating with streams of incandescent nebula, did not dry his eyes. The heavens were beautiful, the spectacle of the alien city spread out before them overwhelming—even Jessa was prettier than ever. But he felt none of it belonged to him. Nothing. And he wondered if he would ever find the feeling of belonging again.

14

Aliens came, people—they wanted to know what had happened. Smoke poured up from the elevator shaft behind them. They stood on a wide green lawn, towers the color of ivory dominating the horizon. Mark and Jessa explained that they didn't know. Authorities appeared minutes later in sphere-shaped silver craft and questioned them further. They wore tight red one-piece uniforms and carried assorted instruments. The interrogation was friendly and civilized. It wasn't the nature of these people, Mark saw, to seek out a place to lay blame. The consensus was formed that the facility's central computer had malfunctioned. What race had been wiped out? Lartza—Mark—told them it was M-1-26-5. Oh, the Terra system, they responded when they consulted their instruments, very primitive.

No one seemed too upset.

Lartza and Dween were told they could go.

Simple as that. Mark was stunned.

They rode what appeared to be a cylindrical phone booth home. It was how they traveled home every day. They stepped into a booth together— the booths were conveniently located every- where—and the contraption locked tight, rose into the sky, and slid into a magnetic slipstream that doubled as the fast lane of a freeway. They merely had to tell the thing where they wanted to go. There was a slight sense of motion. When the door reopened, they were able to step directly into their tiny sterile living room. Apparently every apart- ment had a docking device. Their cylindrical phone booth waited outside.

Home sweet home. They looked at each other and burst out laughing, tension pouring out of them. They had done it, and they couldn't believe it. At least Mark couldn't, he suspected Jessa had known from the beginning that they would win. There was a coldness inside her, at her core, a hand over her light. Today had been a game for her, and he wished he had never cried in front of her.

The aliens—they called themselves the Cray— were not gifted in interior design. The apartment was white and shiny, not much different from an ultra-modern apartment in rich Manhattan. Yet there were alien basics that humanity had only seen in sci-fi movies. Most notable was the food duplicator. It made all their meals—say goodbye to stoves and refrigerators. Mark asked Jessa if she was hungry. She winked and said, yeah, for love. They still had not had sex—not that he could remember. She wanted to try out her new body, on him, and he wasn't opposed. Maybe she was right about his preference, blondes were nice. He moved close and she came closer.

The door opened just then and in walked a blond little girl.

"Hello," she said matter-of-factly. "You two are home early."

Six-year-old Sharmti, their daughter. Very pretty, Mark thought, confused by the delight he felt in seeing her. How much of the Cray man did he carry in his heart? Memories were the glue of emotion, and he could remember the day his daughter had been born. He wanted to hug her, but she went straight for the food duplicator. Mark glanced at Jessa and had to smile at her discomfort. Not the motherly type, his girlfriend. If their daughter knew what was going through her mind, she would have run screaming from the apartment.

"There was an accident at work," Mark said in what must have been his best Cray voice because Sharmti noticed nothing strange in his accent. "We'll be home the rest of the day."

"Your father and I are planning a vacation," Jessa said. "We need privacy."

Sharmti had ordered herself up what looked like

a fruit salad. Mark was surprised to see a diced apple and banana on the plate. Perhaps the Cray had planted the fruit on Earth. Other items, like a blue pear-shaped delicacy, he did not recognize. Their daughter ate as she sat and stared at them.

"Where are we going?" she asked calmly.

"Yes," Mark said. "Where are we going?"

Jessa touched his arm. "We talked about it, dear. We're going on a long trip, off world."

Sharmti showed interest. Her cute little nose wrinkled up. "That is good, I want to do that. Can I free up a study sequence?"

"No," Jessa said.

"Yes," Mark said.

Jessa quietly glared. "What?"

He shrugged. "She is our daughter."

Jessa spoke to Sharmti. "Darling, could you go play outside?"

Sharmti continued to eat. "Why?"

"Because I want you to," Jessa said.

"Why?"

Mark took Jessa's arm. "We're going to talk in our room. We will be out in a few minutes."

"Can we go to Lyra?" Sharmti asked.

"No," Jessa said.

"We'll see," Mark said as he led Jessa into the bedroom and hit the button that closed the door. It was like the living room, devoid of design, but the bed was large and firm. Jessa sat on the edge and growled.

"What the hell do you think you're doing?" she demanded.

"What am I doing? What are you doing? We never discussed taking a trip off world."

"Because we haven't had a chance to discuss it. But it's the next obvious step."

"Obvious to whom?" he asked.

"We can't stay here. These are the creeps who wiped out humanity. We have to get home."

Mark gasped. "What?"

"I thought you knew we would try for Earth. Where else would you want to go?"

"But Earth is four hundred light-years away." He paused and consulted Lartza's memories. "Only their most powerful ships are capable of traveling that distance."

"Then we have to get one of those ships."

"Just like that?" he asked.

"They have nothing to stop us. I have studied this woman's memories. We can rent a small space cruiser to go on a personal vacation to one of their local moons. Once in space, we can hijack one of their military cruisers."

"I'm sure their crew will enjoy that."

"We will kill the crew," Jessa said flatly.

"You're not serious."

Jessa held his eye. "You should know me better than that by now."

Mark paced in front of her. "When did you decide all this?"

"When you walked into my dressing room."

"Bullshit."

"Truth."

He stopped. "This will never work. If one of their cruisers takes off for deep space, they'll go after it."

"No. I have an insight into these people you don't. Remember, I studied them two years. They are autonomous and well behaved, which creates unique social dynamics. No one will go after a cruiser that takes off because none of them would be able to imagine that the captain or crew would do anything unethical. These people don't do such things, and the Cray are so advanced that they have no known galactic enemies. Plus, we will only hijack a cruiser when we are far from this world. We'll give them no warning. We will broadcast their form of SOS, and when they stop to pick us up, you will fry their brains."

"Crazy. Neither of us can pilot such a ship."

"Their computer will pilot it. We merely tell it to go to Earth—or M-1-26-5 as they call it—and it will go there. We will be in hibernation most of the way."

"Abduct an alien vessel, kill the highly trained crew, and take a nap for four centuries. No big deal. What did you have for breakfast this morning?"

"We have to be bold, Mark. Boldness has served us well so far. We would still be rotting in those tanks if we hadn't acted quickly and with strength."

"What about Sharmti?" he asked.

"What about her? We leave her here."

"That will look suspicious. We have to take her with us."

"No. If we take her with us, we'll have to kill her along with the crew."

Mark snorted. "You're not going to kill a little girl."

Jessa stood and grabbed his shoulders. "She's not a little girl. She's not our daughter. She's a murdering bitch from a race of murderers." She stopped. "But you might be right, we might be forced to take her. But be clear in your mind about one thing. If it comes to a choice between her and us, she loses. There's no way we take her to Earth."

For once, Mark believed Jessa was taking the tough-chick routine too far. She was his girlfriend, her outlandish ideas blew his mind every few minutes, but he was sure she was not capable of hurting a little girl. He convinced himself that he knew that much about her.

"I will consider your plan," he said.

She let go of him. "Consider it quickly. I want to leave tomorrow."

"Is that an order, boss?" he asked.

"The longer we stay here, the more we'll stand out."

"I said, I'll think about it."

Jessa glanced at the closed door. "Do you think she can hear?"

"Sort of late to ask that question, don't you think?"

Jessa smiled and touched his chest. "Do you want to do it?"

"With Sharmti in the next room?"

Jessa was disgusted. "To hell with Sharmti." She turned away.

Mark sighed. "Lucky for us I never had a little sister."

184

15

That night Mark helped Sharmti get ready for bed. He tucked her in; she seemed to expect it and, besides, he thought it a nice gesture. She was a precocious child but sweet as well. He enjoyed watching her study her three-dimensional holographically projected school lessons that evening. Six years old and already learning physics and chemistry. He was the doting father, impressed.

Jessa was in the other room, at the computer terminal, pouring over the Cray equivalent of the Internet. Naturally both he and Jessa had volumes of latent memories on what was involved in obtaining a personal ship for local space travel. Jessa said she was brushing up on the fine points of rental— go figure. The Cray society had no concept of money. They could use what they wished; they merely had to ask for it. Jessa had already put in a request for the most powerful personal spaceship on the computer. Takeoff was scheduled for early the next day.

Mark felt they were moving too fast.

Yet there was wisdom in Jessa's course. They had already been notified, via their computer, that they were to appear at a special commission that would meet in two days to try to reconstruct what had gone wrong at the brain-warming facility. Mark could see that their simple denials would not continue to fly. It was possible they could be detained, although the Crays appeared to have no jails. Jessa said they could not go to that meeting and, for once, Mark had to agree.

Sharmti wanted to know their destination as she snuggled into bed. Mark sat beside her, close to her head. He had helped her brush and dry her long hair after her shower. She had seemed to expect that. From introspection he knew that even the real Lartza was closer to his daughter than Dween was. Mark smiled at her question.

"Why don't we let it be a surprise," he said.

"But I don't like surprises. They're not logical. Where are we going?"

He hesitated. "To Lyra."

Her blue eyes shone with pleasure. "Can I ride a Burta Bear once we get there?"

"Of course. I'll ride one with you."

The idea excited her. "But you're too big for a Burta Bear. Why don't you ride a Gongo Skip while I ride the Burta Bear?"

"OK. Have it your way." He paused. "What else do you want to do there?"

She thought. "We can go to the ice caves and let the Spy Chilies bite us."

He grimaced. "Won't that hurt?"

She giggled. "No, silly, their venom will make us laugh."

He checked that fact with Lartza's memories. He messed up her hair and reached for the light. "You go to sleep. We have a long day tomorrow." As he stood, she took his hand.

"Father?"

"Yes?"

"Is there something wrong with Mother?"

"Why?"

"She's acting strange."

"Oh, you know your mother—she is strange."

Sharmti smiled and kissed his hand. "I love you, Father."

He was touched, despite himself. "I love you, Sharmti."

Mark turned off the light and left the room, closing the door behind him. Jessa was still at the computer, which projected its images directly into the space in front of her. But she turned it off as he approached, as if she didn't want him seeing what she was researching.

"How is the little beast?" she asked.

"She thinks you're strange."

"Really? Me? I never saw a child who stares so much."

"You might want to give her more attention. You're raising unnecessary suspicions in her mind."

"You might want to give her less attention. I see that you're getting attached to her and I don't understand it."

He sat down across from her and shrugged. "She's a sweet kid; it's no big deal."

Jessa stared out the wide window and he followed her lead. Both suns were gone. The sky blazed with nebulae, and the spaceport glowed like, well, an alien city. They were ninety-four stories up. The view was incredible, and Mark was pleased that they had come at least this far. He wasn't hopeful that the next phase of their plan would work. His wild gift felt like a tumor in his skull, one he wasn't anxious to unleash again. Yet he felt no alternative but to go along with Jessa's plan, for now.

"You're right," Jessa said quietly. "She's no big deal."

He wanted to change the subject. "I bet we made Mr. Grimes happy."

Jessa shook her head. "I'm sure he never had a chance to experience happiness, not after what we did." She glanced at him. "But you don't like to think about it."

"I can deal with it. Besides, you were the one who talked about the need to run away two days ago."

She nodded. "To run all the way back to Earth would be the biggest escape." She whispered to herself, "Everything's backward."

"What?"

She shook herself. "Just thinking aloud. Did you know we don't even have to pack? The ship we've been allotted will have everything we need on board."

"Good. I have no luggage."

She smiled at him, sad at the edges though. "Are you tired?"

"A little. You?"

"A bit. Want to go to bed?"

"Should have asked me that when we met."

"I would have scared you away." She lost her smile. "I do scare you, don't I?"

He hesitated. "Not in the way you think."

"How then?"

He strove to be honest but was confused. "I feel there are parts of you I know very well. Only I can't remember those parts."

"That makes sense," she said.

He shook his head. "Nothing about our situation makes sense. Do you ever stop to think about that?"

"No. I keep moving forward. That's all I can do."

"You sound like a realist. Why those comments about running away?"

The question disturbed her. "What is real?"

"I hope you are. I don't want to be in love with someone who isn't."

His remark meant a lot to her. "Do you really love me?"

"Sure."

"Say it."

"I love you," he said.

She struggled with unexpected pain. He saw tears form in her eyes, and it shocked him. Her gaze flew out the window. "I can't keep you," she said.

He chuckled. "You have to keep me. I have to keep you. We don't have a whole lot of choice here." He paused. "Jessa?"

The fingers on her right hand fluttered for him to stop. "It's nothing. I'm just worried about tomorrow."

He stood. "I am, too, and we need to rest, so let's go to bed."

She looked up at him with hope. "Will you love me?"

He offered his hands. "Sure."

She hesitated. "Will you love me forever? No matter what I do?"

He wanted to say yes. She needed his yes.

But he didn't answer. He couldn't lie.

16

MAGIC FIRE

The blastoff from Cray was completely uneventful. At the spaceport they were directed to a room where they waited alone. Finally a door opened. They walked inside, sat down in a circular room, and—without realizing it—took off into outer space. There was no sense of motion, no sound. The craft didn't open its side windows until they were high above the planet.

The view from orbit was stunning. Cray appeared much like Earth seen from the space shuttle, but with even more water. Mark marveled at the interplay of the red and yellow suns on the glistening seas. He knew this world—it was his host's home, after all—yet he felt that he had assimilated little of the culture. They had seen the blue tanks, the violet generator, the wide lawn outside the brain facility, the sterile apartment.

Their hasty walk through the spaceport had been restricted to escalators and elevators. He knew he should curse the people and planet below, but he longed to know them. Why had they done what they did to Earth? Now he supposed he would never understand.

Of course they still had Sharmti.

Jessa directed the ship out of orbit in the direction of Lyra, the fifth moon of a gaseous giant at the edge of the Cray solar system. Sharmti watched as she set the course, delighted at the thought of seeing the Burta Bears soon. The duration of the flight was to be six hours. Mark knew Jessa would make a major course correction long before Lyra. Jessa simply wanted to make it appear that they were heading toward the vacation moon. Vessel traffic in and around Cray was heavy. These people traveled in space on the weekends as Earthmen sailed the seas. So much freedom. Mark wondered if their spoiled sensibilities had made them immune to the pain they caused other races.

Well on their way, Jessa ordered Sharmti to her room. Go study your holograms, get out of our faces. Sharmti was agreeable and danced off to look at tapes of Burta Bears. Mark laughed as she left; Jessa scowled.

"Don't grow too fond of her," she warned.

"You're not going to hurt her."

"I'm not going to help her. Neither are you, she is the enemy."

"Somehow she doesn't look like the enemy to me."

Jessa sat in the navigator's chair and looked around for something.

"What is it?" he asked.

"I want a cigarette."

"When we get to Earth you can have one."

She frowned. "Don't you miss them?"

"I told you, I don't smoke." But the words were no sooner out of his mouth than he felt a craving for one. Odd, she must be using her witchy powers on him again.

"We will have to steer this ship into the military lanes. But I want to wait until we are outside the solar system. Agreed?"

"Fine. But what if the computer refuses to take us into the lanes?"

She hadn't thought of that. "It could override the command?"

"Sure. I would have designed it that way if I were a Cray, as a safety precaution." He considered Lartza's memories. "It could be a problem. We might have to disable the computer, steer it manually."

"I'd rather not have to do it."

"We might not have a choice."

She nodded. "Whatever it takes."

"Your personal motto?"

"Sure. I hope you're not suffering from your

nonviolent attitude toward the Cray this morning?"

"You expect me to get used to murder?" he asked.

"It's not murder; it's defense. There's a difference."

"Not when they die because of something I've done."

"You haven't seen any of them die," she said.

"Have you? Were you able to kill a few while in your out-of-body state?"

"You know I don't have your gift," she said.

He wasn't convinced.

"Do you miss your MAZE?" he asked.

"No."

"It meant so much to you."

"I never put it in my brain until all I had left was my brain."

"Does the Cray invasion make all our acts in the last ten years insignificant?"

"I don't know. Does it make you feel better about the fire you lit in Pacific Palisades?"

She was in a feisty mood, but her question was a good one.

"It does make me feel better," he admitted. "No one really died."

"How about your mother's death?"

His mood darkened. "I don't want to talk about that."

She nodded. "Now you know why I don't want to talk about MAZE."

He didn't see the connection but let it be.

Sharmti wandered in and out of the control room. She kept asking if they were there yet. Jessa put her off; the reality was they were way past *there*. Jessa had altered their course without difficulty. Right into the military lanes—the ship's computer had not protested. Mark was surprised, but what did he know.

Sharmti finally lay down to sleep, after accepting their explanation that their ship was a slow one. Mark told her a bedtime story—Cinderella and the Seven Dwarfs. He blended the characters of both stories together. He let Cinderella die in the end—which Sharmti hated—by having one of the wicked dwarfs cut out Cinderella's heart. He wasn't very good at putting kids to bed. Still, Sharmti fell asleep while he was in the room, and he sat and watched her soft breathing for several minutes. He couldn't explain his deep attachment to the child. Acknowledging Lartza's memories buried inside his brain, Mark still felt there was more to it than that.

Four hours after Sharmti lay down to sleep, just when Jessa and Mark were thinking of getting a few hours' sleep, their long-range scans picked up a huge ship speeding home toward Cray. The alien suns were now nothing but bright stars shimmering in an ocean of galactic dust. Jessa paced the control room and acted as if she wanted to sound battle stations. She ordered Mark to get out of the control chair but was too high strung to sit down herself.

"We have to send them an SOS," she said.

He stood. "Do it."

"I don't know how to word it."

"Tell them to hurry and get here. We're about to explode."

"Will they believe that?" she asked.

"I don't know."

"You don't know? We have to get this right."

"Why would we lie to them? You said it yourself, no one lies in this society."

Fretting, Jessa sat in the control chair. She instructed the computer to open an emergency line to the approaching vessel. A moment later they heard from the Cray. The voice was that of a no-nonsense female. Sounded like military to Mark.

"This is the Star Cruiser Helon 77T. Please state the nature of your emergency?"

Jessa spoke into the equivalent of the ship's microphone. "We're not sure what is wrong, Helon. We are losing atmosphere. Can you rescue us within the next hour?"

"What are your technical readings?"

Jessa glanced at Mark.

"Tell them that all systems outside of communications have failed," he said.

Jessa conveyed the message. The Helon was a long time responding. Finally they reported that they were changing course to intercept. Jessa breathed a sigh of relief.

"We're safe now," she said.

"We're far from safe," Mark replied, feeling dread with what was to come.

The Helon did not show for more than an hour, but then its approach was breathtaking. A featureless silver sphere—it swept in at blinding speed and swelled overhead until it appeared to be as large as a moon. Mark estimated it was more than ten miles in diameter. Its sheer size intimidated him out of any desire to use his gift on its crew. But Jessa was adamant he do it.

"The moment we dock," she said, "you must kill them all."

He shook his head. "There could be a million people on that ship."

"It doesn't make any difference."

"How am I supposed to do this? I can't even see them. I'll cause the ship to explode like the blue tanks."

Jessa shook her head. The military cruiser descended on them like a mountain on an ant. A black door opened on the bottom of its smooth surface, and their tiny vessel was jerked upward and towed toward the cruiser.

"I'll take you out of your body," she said, "then we can sweep their corridors. Do what you did to Dr. Brain. Burn out their cortexes."

"Then we just stroll in?"

"We have no choice."

"We always have a choice."

She was cold. "Sit down and close your eyes. Let's get this over with."

He wanted to protest more, but knew she was right about the time. It pressed on him more than her because he felt they must finish their dirty deed before Sharmti awoke. He swore that she was not going to see all the dead bodies. They would hide them away, or else carry her to her room with a blanket over her head. She could not know what her parents had changed into.

Who was the enemy?

Mark was beginning to wonder.

They slipped inside the giant ship.

He closed his eyes and breathed. Jessa spoke to him in a soft voice about inner and outer space, the power of the mystical eye, and the endless possibilities of the human nervous system. He clung to his body as he felt himself slip out of it. He saw the moon Lyra where he had promised to take his daughter. He wanted to see the Burta Bears and Gongo Skips and have the Spy Chilies bite him so that he could laugh off what was about to happen. He didn't know the astral body could cry, but dampness clouded his vision. Jessa said a harsh word in a gentle tone, and he felt himself being sucked into a silver ball the size of a beating heart. He was the insect invading their orderly universe.

He swept their hallways, endless and crowded, at

least a million in uniform. A ghost flew beside him, not white and innocent as an angel, but dark as the Grim Reaper. The unseen fire shimmered in the space between them, and he knew this time he wouldn't be able to control it.

The Cray began to scream.

Fire caught fire. It invaded nostrils, crawled through ears, exploded eyeballs. The Cray pressed their hands over their faces as if to pray for mercy, but he had inadvertently summoned a force that showed no compassion. They whirled and crashed into one another as their blood splattered the walls and drenched the floor. Their tongues smoked; their agony was a nightmare. No, they didn't die as Dr. Brain had died, although Mark feverishly prayed that they would. The Magic Fire lived, and it let him know it had its own desires. These were the enemy, it told him, a line he had heard somewhere before. They would perish as it saw fit.

Beside him, the Reaper was flying through bloody flame.

Mark thought he saw her grin.

17

They sat in silence in their small ship a long time after their return to their bodies. The lights in the control room had mysteriously dimmed. No one called to them from the great vessel, but Mark thought he heard their ghosts weep. A curse repaid with a curse. How many aboard the Helon had even heard of Earth?

"I don't want Sharmti to see," he whispered finally.

"I agree. We cannot take her aboard."

He jerked. "We cannot leave her here."

"Yes. We can leave her asleep and jettison this small ship. She'll be picked up eventually."

"You don't know that for sure."

"No. But it's the reasonable thing to do."

"What is reasonable about leaving a six-year-old

child alone in deep space? She will wake up—not find us—and become terrified."

"Mark," Jessa said patiently, "there were thousands of Cray children aboard the Helon. They're all dead now."

He was bitter. "So what is one more?"

"I'm not a monster. You might be surprised to hear that I've come to like her as well. Not as you like her, of course, but in my own way. I honestly think she will be safe if we jettison her in this ship. We are in the lanes. See how quickly the Helon appeared. I can set the computer to emit a constant SOS."

Her reasoning was sound. It would be cruel to force Sharmti to go to Earth when all she knew was Cray, but Mark was tired of Jessa's reasons. They appeared to be right, but they felt wrong. He didn't want to leave Sharmti because he cared for her and in her mind he was her father. A child could not be separated from her parents, he told himself. It was not human.

"No," he said.

"Mark . . ."

He stood. "No, I won't leave her."

She stared up at him. "But we can't bring her to Earth."

"Then I will stay with her in this ship and bring her back to Cray. You go to Earth, I'll come later."

"That's insane. It's four hundred light-years to Earth. Even at light speed, it will take the Helon four centuries to get there. What are you going to do? Catch up?"

He shook his head. "I draw the line here."

She stood slowly. "You're making a mistake."

"I've made them before."

"Like when you decided to get to know me?"

"I didn't say that," he snapped.

"You would really leave me for her?"

He hesitated. "Yes."

Jessa's lower lip trembled. "Very well, I'm glad to know where I stand in your universe. I guess she comes with us to Earth." She stepped past him toward the escape hatch. "When she wakes up, you explain the bloody corpses to her."

Mark sweated. "What if they're not all dead?"

Jessa would not look at him. "Believe me, they are."

Sharmti continued to sleep. Jessa and Mark boarded the Helon. There were bodies everywhere, the stench awful. He tried not to look, but that was a worse mistake—to accidentally kick a warm body, feel it roll. Faint red vapor wafted above ruined mouths, the bloody steam of unimaginable death. None of them had known what was killing them. Mark tried to play a Jessa argument in his own head. No one on Earth knew when civilization had halted; therefore, this was justified.

The justification sounded tired and worn.

He realized he was getting tired of his girlfriend, but that didn't mean he loved her any less. He worried that he was capable of watching her kill an entire planet and still love her. Ebo came to mind then. He would die if she died in his arms—let the curtain fall. They breathed in rhythm—the blue fluid had welded their brains together. He had finally lied to her. He doubted he could have abandoned her to stay with Sharmti.

Sharmti, though. She did matter a great deal.

Jessa went off to search for the control room. He found a clean quarters—i.e., one without a body in it—and hurried to fetch Sharmti. She slept deeply and only stirred slightly as he lifted her up to carry her on board the Helon. The new bed was the same as the old for her. He kissed her on the forehead and tried to figure out a way to keep her in the room until they went into hibernation.

Jessa reappeared in a hallway strewn with bodies.

"We have to be careful not to get lost," he said.

"The ship's computer can tell you where you are at all times."

"Did you find the control room?" he asked.

"Yes. I told the computer to take us to M-1-26-5—maximum speed." She beamed. "We're on our way home, Mark."

"They might follow us."

"Unlikely. I checked the specs on this ship. It is one of the ten fastest in their fleet. The other nine are all off on deep-space missions. Plus I found out something else. This ship is equipped with a staff of ten thousand robots. I've instructed them to take all the bodies down to engineering and incinerate them in the reactor."

"I haven't seen any of these robots," Mark said.

"I bumped into a couple. They look vaguely humanoid but have metallic skin. They are polite but not very bright. The Cray may have limited their intelligence on purpose. I seem to remember something like that from Dween's memories."

"Speaking of Dween, we have to start calling each other by our Cray names in front of Sharmti."

"No," Jessa said. "I won't do that, not once we reach Earth. She'll adapt to our real names."

"It's a small thing to ask," Mark said.

"No. It's a big thing. It cuts to the core of who we are."

This was how it would be between them, he realized. He had dared to say no to Jessa, to place Sharmti's life over his love of her. She would always resent him even while loving him. How tragic to have divisiveness between them when they were such a small family in such a big galaxy.

"Have it your way then." He added, "Jessa."

She ignored the sarcasm. "Where is Sharmti?"

He gestured. "Down the hall—asleep in somebody's quarters."

"We can move her to a hibernation chamber if you want."

He nodded. "I think we should all go under right away."

"You don't want to wait to see if we're pursued?"

"You just said we wouldn't be."

"We can err on the side of safety," she said.

"It makes no difference. If they catch us we're screwed."

"Not with you aboard."

He spoke abruptly. "I won't do that again."

"Even if they open fire on us?"

"Never."

She saw that he was serious. "OK. Let the robots clear a clean path to the hibernation chambers and you bring Sharmti. We can all go to sleep together." She brightened. "Just think, when we wake up, Earth will be in the sky."

"Will we recognize it?" he wondered aloud.

His comment darkened her mood.

"It will be all ours," she said firmly.

Three robots appeared before Mark could get to Sharmti. Their movements were rather stiff and they had tin for complexions, but they were friendly and worked fast. They didn't even ask why all the Cray had died. Mark suspected Jessa was right—the Cray had made them with simple minds so they couldn't compete with them.

When Sharmti woke up she was excited that they were on such a big ship.

"What happened?" she asked as Mark carried her toward the hibernation chamber. The three expressionless robots walked on either side.

"We've been asked by our government to go on a

very important mission," he said. "We are taking this big ship and leaving the solar system for a planet far away."

She wrinkled her nose. "We won't get to see the Burta Bears?"

"No, but the planet we're going to is very beautiful, and we will be the only ones there."

That interested her. "But what will we do there?"

"Have lots of fun. You'll see."

The hibernation chamber area was vast, endless white coffins laid out for a crew who no longer needed them. They reminded him of the tombs of the ancient Egyptians. He was disgusted to see that many of the crew had been in deep sleep when they had been attacked. The instruments on their elongated boxes said they were all dead, as if he needed the readings. A closer examination showed blood splattered against the clear plates above their contorted faces. He steered Sharmti away from such chambers.

Jessa was their new chief engineer, and she seemed to revel in the role, programming the computer, ordering the robots about. Three clean chambers waited for them when Mark walked in with Sharmti. Jessa put the child down and told her not to fuss.

"But I just slept," Sharmti said. "I can't sleep now."

"You will sleep," Jessa said. "The box will put

you to sleep." She began to lower the hatch. Mark stopped her.

"Kiss her good night," he said.

Jessa leaned over and gave Sharmti a kiss. The little girl hugged her mother. Jessa tried not to show it, but Mark caught the warm glow on her face. It gave him hope.

Two minutes later Sharmti was unconscious.

Mark climbed into his chamber.

He looked around for a heart monitor.

Of course there was nothing so primitive.

Jessa hugged him as he tried to get comfortable. Four hundred and twenty years, wow—he would have quite a beard by then. He hoped he would wake up with his brain in his body. He did feel excited at the prospect of seeing Earth again, but tried not to show it. His attitude was "one day at a time, hope little and try to suffer the least possible." He was not going to sleep with a clear conscience and wondered if he would have sweet dreams. He hugged Jessa back but not as hard as he would have a week earlier. She sensed his coolness and drew back.

"It'll be OK," she said.

"I know you've been trying your best."

She swallowed. His remark had stung.

"I just had this fantasy of being alone with you," she said.

"Even Adam and Eve had children."

She nodded tightly. "I'll try to be nice to her. I do like her, really."

"I know you do. Jessa?"

"Yes?"

He hesitated. "Nothing. You have sweet dreams."

She gave him a quick kiss. "You, too."

The hatch closed. He stretched out and took slow deep breaths. A gust of cold air blew up from his feet, a faint chemical smell touched his nose, and in the space of time that he blinked a wave of drowsiness swept over him. He thought of Adam and Eve, Cain and Abel. Outside his face plate it grew dark. He fell asleep trying to remember which brother had killed the other.

18

The blue ball in the black sky looked little different. The chronometer said it was the thirtieth century. They directed the computer to bring the Helon down in the Pacific Palisades area. They were surprised to see that the entire West Side was a small island off the California coast. The big quake had finally hit. Too bad there was no one around to collect the insurance premiums. Even with the landscape rearranged, Jessa and Mark recognized home. Their star cruiser settled gracefully above the Malibu beach where Jessa and he had gone on their first date. It hovered two feet off the ground without making a sound as it cast a vast shadow over the land.

Exiting through a simple hatch, they felt a warm wind blow off the ocean. The waves and sand hadn't changed, but there were no lifeguard stations, only the ghosts of homes on the Malibu hills, the latter flatter and more weary than they remembered. Sharmti skipped along the beach, happy to be in a natural environment. Mark turned to Jessa.

"It'll be OK," she repeated.

He gestured. "The waves aren't so big. We can go body surfing."

She chuckled. "You were a coward that day."

"And you were only brave because you knew you couldn't get hurt."

She nodded and took his hand. "It's the same now. This is our world. The Cray will never dream to search for their missing ship here. Nothing can hurt us."

He wanted to be happy. In a sense he had all he ever wanted, certainly more than he possessed that Friday night when he stepped into her dressing room. But a sense of sadness had not been released from him during the long hibernation. He had not dreamed, of course, yet now he was plagued by thoughts of the Garden of Eden. The serpent and the tree of knowledge. He worried that he would find such an apple, bite into it, and his paradise would shatter. But not because Jessa would force the fruit on him. Indeed, he suspected she knew where the apple grew, and that she would do everything in her power to keep it from him.

They explored, the three of them, a handful of robots always nearby to help. The elements had destroyed most homes, but some of the larger buildings were occasionally salvageable piles, places they could sleep in, make into a home, if they so desired. Of course the Helon was an easy residence—wind and rain never pierced its hull. Mark worried that such a safe haven made them lazy and Jessa agreed, wanting to send the ship and robots out of the solar system, as soon as they could live without them. He admired her courage and feared it as well. Even canned food, which existed in abundance beneath the rubble, was completely rotten.

No matter, Jessa said. They could plant and hunt. There were animals everywhere: deer, dogs, rabbits, mountain lions, and bears—Sharmti loved to watch them. Mark never let her get too close to them and never let her out alone. Besides keeping robots close by, he always carried a deadly blaster that could take out a whole building when set at full power.

Jessa was foolishly brave—careless, he thought. She didn't want Cray technology around and hiked alone without robots or weapons. Mark scolded her: what if a brown bear attacks you? You have a body now, not just a brain. She laughed and said she could take care of herself.

She took him in her arms whenever they were alone outside the ship. She loved to make love in warm and ruined basements best. They had sex several times a day, and in that sense it was paradise for both of them. They never talked about babies or birth control. Odd, he thought.

Still, the apple. He knew it was there.

He found it the day Sharmti died.

They had been home three months. Summer was turning into winter—autumn had departed with humanity. A cold breeze blew down from the north. The waves crashed thick and angry against the shore. They had never left their West Side island. Why bother?

An omen should have alerted him to the danger, but he failed to see it. Leaving the Helon—which still hovered over Malibu Beach—early in the morning he found Jessa and Sharmti preparing to take off on a long hike. At his insistence Jessa had a blaster with her but no robots. The black weapon rode high on her sexy hip. Sharmti chased birds into the water. Jessa had a cigarette in her mouth, smoking up a storm. She offered him one, and he took it without thinking.

"Where did you get these?" he asked.

She puffed, nicotine heaven. "Found a halfway decent carton buried under the Getty Museum. Had a Van Gogh on top of it."

"Did you save the painting?"

"No. Tore through it to get to the cigarettes." She offered him a light—Bic had survived the ages. He waved away the orange flame.

"Where are you going today?" he asked.

"Where the mood takes us," Jessa said. "Want to come?"

He yawned. "No. I think I'll take it easy today. There's some reading I want to catch up on."

She was curious. "What are you reading?"

"Your unpublished novel. Finally found it."

She did not smile. He kissed them both goodbye.

Jessa was back five hours later, carrying Sharmti's body. They had been exploring the precarious ruins of Santa Monica pier, a place he had forbidden them to walk. But Sharmti had been dying to touch what was left of the Ferris wheel, so Jessa had taken her out over the broken asphalt and twisted girders. Sharmti had slipped and fallen into the water. Before Jessa could dive in to rescue her, a large wave dashed the girl's head against a concrete pillar. Jessa thought she had died instantly.

Mark held Sharmti as Jessa explained. The little girl was so cold, but the blue tanks had been warm. He didn't understand how both could be true. The apple was rotten to the core, and it tasted bitter as he buried his face in his daughter's chest.

But he didn't weep, he couldn't.

He built a funeral pyre for Sharmti on top of the hill where he had started the fire to burn his hometown to the ground. The robots helped with the pyre, but he sent them away before speaking his final words. The long goodbye. He was not a minister and didn't know how these things were supposed to go. Jessa stayed close by his side and wept quietly. He didn't believe for an instant that she had wished Sharmti dead—he couldn't believe that and live. Not in what was supposed to be paradise.

He had not cleared away the dry shrubs from beside the pyre. When it burned, much else would burn. The wind had picked up, and now it blew fierce, cold, and dry. If they were not careful the entire island might go up. He removed a lighter from his pocket, flicked it hard, and held the flame before him. No unnatural power disturbed his mind. The Magic Fire was dead. Without speaking, he touched the flame to the dry wood and stepped back. The flames caught and slipped up over Sharmti's tiny form, smothering what was left of his hopes. He wanted to turn away when her hair caught fire but found he could not.

The tears—still, they would not come.

Jessa tugged at his side. "We don't have to stay."

"But we do," he said. The supernatural clarity of emptiness settled over his soul. He remembered Buddha had said that the seed of bondage was desire. His bindings burned with Sharmti. He felt strangely free, able to see their desolate world from a new angle. Smoke blew in his face, but he didn't move. Even when Jessa cried and asked him not to make her watch.

"It disturbs you?" he asked. "I thought you had the strong stomach."

She misunderstood. "You blame me?"

"No." He shook his head. "Never."

"Mark?"

"Do you have a cigarette?" he asked suddenly.

"No. Not on me."

"Too bad."

"Why?" she asked.

He stared at the massive bulk of the floating Helon, its shadow blanketing them. The alien star cruiser from the depths of the galaxy, the ark of the heavens. He thought of the Bible; they should have found one and read prayers for Sharmti. Sections from Genesis. The snake—he couldn't stop thinking about how one taste of the fruit of knowledge had destroyed the garden. Fire crept over Sharmti's face. He held the mythical apple in his hand and squeezed it to see if it was ripe. It was all he needed for lunch; he didn't care about the consequences.

The Buddha had another wise saying.

Enlightenment was merely the memory of what always was.

Mark understood it all in an instant.

"There is no way a carton of cigarettes could have survived for eight centuries," he said after a long pause.

"What are you talking about?"

He looked at her. "You wanted one so bad. On Cray you obviously couldn't have one because it wouldn't make sense that they would smoke. But here . . . Jessa, here, you made a mistake."

She shook her head slightly. "I don't know what you mean."

"I believe you don't, and I think that's the way of it. You couldn't enjoy it if you knew it wasn't real." He stopped. "I often wondered why everything worked out so easily for us."

"You mean our escape? That wasn't easy. We were lucky."

"I don't believe in luck," he said.

She had a tic in her right eye, which gave away how nervous she was. Taking his arm, she tried to pull him farther from the fire. But he shook her off; he liked the smoke in his face and wasn't worried that he'd be burned. She trembled as she took a step back. Tear tracks streaked her face.

"We can't stay here, Mark. Let's go back. It's getting late."

"Yeah. It's very late."

She shook her head. "Are you sure you don't blame me?"

"I'm sure, Jessa."

"Then what is it? Why are you acting this way?"

He studied her face. Even in an alien body he could see her as she had looked when he first stepped in that dressing room: the gray eyes, the sensual mouth. That had not been centuries ago, but only two years in the past. Two real years. He had fallen in love with her, watching her onstage.

"We never saw much of Cray," he said. "Only

tiny bits, facades—the scenery reminded me of just that, theatrical scenery and props. Your imagination couldn't fill in the details. Maybe mine couldn't, either. There was just enough there to convince me. The compound was simple—a few square buildings in the desert. Even Mr. Grimes and Dr. Brain were easy—I could have written their characters." He stopped. "Of course you're the novelist."

Her demeanor changed, becoming both removed and fearful.

A tremor shook her body. The smoke felt cold.

"Don't," she whispered. "Please don't."

"I'm sorry, I must do it for you. I came here for you."

The strength went out of her. She fell to her knees in front of him, clasped his hand, and kissed it anxiously. Her eyes stared up at his with such longing that it broke his heart to have to do this to her. Just words, the snake whispered in his ear. That was all it took. He had to listen to his own conscience because he was as trapped as she was.

No, that wasn't true.

She was the one on her knees who was begging.

"Don't say any more," she pleaded.

"I must."

"But we can be happy here! We are happy!"

He glanced at Sharmti. The flames had her.

He sighed. "There's no happiness here for either of us." He pulled her to her feet and gazed deeply into her haunted eyes. He forced the words into her mind and held a mirror up to her face. He had to shatter her illusion. "You called this planet M-1-26-5. Do you know what that spells?"

She shook her head and wanted to plug her ears.

"1 is A. 26 is Z. 5 is E. I know the alphabet, you see." He paused, thoughtful. "But I don't know if that was you telling me or me telling me."

She swallowed painfully. "MAZE is a drug."

"No." He gestured. "All this is MAZE. All this is a prison."

She blinked. "I can't go back."

"You have to go back. I won't stay here with you."

Tears burst out from her—she was so wounded. "You would leave me all alone?"

He knew he had to be firm; it killed him.

"I'm going to leave you." His heart ached. "Come with me. There's nothing for you here."

She turned her back on him and stared out to sea.

The shadow from the Helon had vanished.

Still, the fire burned, keeping them warm.

Winter would come hard and fast this year.

"I cannot go back," she said softly. "I've been gone too long. I know nothing else, and there is nothing else I want to know."

Her wound was his wound. Never to heal.

He did love her, he always would.

"The doctors say you will die," he said.

She wouldn't look at him again. "I understand, and it doesn't matter." Her voice cracked but she did not turn back to him. "Goodbye, Mark."

He reached out to touch her.

But his arm wasn't that long.

He didn't get to say goodbye.

Epilogue

Mark Charm heard the heart monitor beep beside his head, but he didn't open his eyes. He had been warned not to do so. There had been no transition, one minute he was on the hilltop with Jessa Welling and now he was lying in a bed in a Mexican clinic, hooked up to the same brain tap that fed into his girlfriend's skull. He waited for the attending physician to come. The man, a compassionate doctor, must be near. He had been anxious to help Mark free Jessa from her MAZE addiction. The newspapers back in the States said these clinics were staffed only by pseudo professionals who only wanted money, but Mark knew that people were people. There was good and bad everywhere. The doctor would come soon.

But it was his sister, Shani, whose voice he heard first.

"Take it easy, Mark," she said. "Keep your eyes closed and don't move. The doctor will be here in a minute to take the tap out of your head."

Mark swallowed, his throat painfully dry.

"I couldn't save her," he whispered.

"Just relax," Shani said. "We can talk later."

Mark felt as if ten minutes went by but wasn't sure. His perception of time was distorted, and he wondered how long he had been under. Finally he heard Dr. John Smyth's reassuring voice, the physician's sure hands on the back of his head. The tap was harder to put in than to remove, but both operations were critical. Mark felt pain at the base and top of his skull just before there was a stinging yank and a trickle of warm blood flowed into his right ear. The doctor dabbed him with rubbing alcohol; the tap was out. A wave of nausea swept over Mark, and he feared he'd vomit. But the sick feeling passed, and the doctor told him that he could open his eyes.

Mark blinked in the dim clinic light. The heart monitor beeped, his chest still hooked up to the machine. Shani and Dr. Smyth stared down at him. Shani looked like an older version of Sharmti, sixteen instead of six. The doctor was a Mexican model of Mr. Grimes. Neither of these things surprised him. To his left, on a similar bed, lay Jessa: a plastic tube in her shrunken stomach to feed her; black wires taped on her bare chest to monitor her vital signs; a silver brain tap sunk in her skull to kill her. But it had been her choice, her choice to escape the world and dream an endless fantasy, he reminded himself. It had cost her, too—her entire inheritance, a cool million. But Mexican law said that she could not be removed from the brain tap without her written permission. The clinic owned her mind and money. Dr. Smyth spoke of quitting and working elsewhere.

The clinic name: **MAZE.**

Mental Alteration Zeitgeist Expansion.

A German invention. Popular everywhere.

It was a brave new world. 2010. MAZE was worse than any drug the twentieth century had cooked up, but all such addictions led to the same grave. The last year of dreaming had been hard on Jessa. She was locked in a malfunctioning Cray hibernation chamber—a shriveled mummy. She was even losing her beautiful dark hair. He felt a tear burn his eye and wiped it away so the others couldn't see. Damn her, he thought.

Why hadn't she come back with him?

Love was not enough for her.

"How do you feel?" Dr. Smyth asked.

"Fine," Mark said quietly.

Shani was worried. "You pierced her veil?"

"Yes."

"But she said no?"

He reached out to touch Jessa's hand goodbye.

"She said no," he replied.

It was another hour before Mark was ready to

leave the clinic. He learned he had been under only six hours. The information staggered him. How many fantasies had Jessa lived in the last year? How many versions of him had she manufactured? But he knew, in the end, that she had known he was the real thing. Still, she had said no. It didn't matter that the answer meant she would die. He had really lost her. He realized that he hadn't accepted the bitter truth until then. He wished he had never driven down from L.A. to the clinic. Still, he had had to try one last time.

Shani didn't want him to drive and took his car keys. He slowly climbed in the passenger seat. He felt stiff and sore; a classic side effect from wrestling another person's demons. The fantasy had been largely Jessa's—she was the expert. Only bits and pieces of him had surfaced—Sharmti and his mother—and Jessa had killed them both.

He was not a pyromaniac, although he loved fires, the careless destruction, the sweet smoke, most of all the heat. Jessa had taken the characteristic and run with it—or run with him. Everything, from the play onward, had been a fantasy. Yet she had kept their meeting the same as it had been in real life. He had really gone to see her perform in *The Season of the Witch,* a story she had written to star in onstage. Now he supposed she would always be a star, in her own lonely universe. A falling star that was destined to burn up in the sky.

He knew he would miss her forever.

"You OK?" Shani asked, still worried.

"Sure," he said.

Mark had a headache and wanted Tylenol—he should have asked for a pill at the clinic. Although his sister hated the things, Shani offered him a cigarette. He took it and searched his pockets for a lighter. He couldn't find one. Shani pulled out of the clinic parking lot. Downtown Tijuana—lovely.

"How's Mom?" he asked as he tried the glove compartment.

"Fine. Why?"

He paused and stared straight ahead. "Jessa wanted to be alone with me in her world. It was important to her."

Shani put a hand on his shoulder. "You did the best you could."

"I know."

"Maybe she'll come out of it on her own."

"No. That will never happen."

"Were you able to tell her how you felt about her?"

"Yes. It didn't matter." He found a lighter, flicked it, and drew it close to his cigarette. A bad habit—Jessa had turned him on to it.

But just before he lit the cigarette, he stopped and put the tip to his forehead. His mystical eye touched the tobacco. He closed his eyes and concentrated. He had been fooled twice today. What was real?

"Now they have total control over the experiment.

They can alter it as they please. They can stop it whenever they want."

"What are you doing?" Shani asked.

He opened his eyes. The cigarette had not lit. He used the lighter on it and drew in a long drag. His headache began to recede.

"Nothing," he said. "Let's go home."

**Coming Soon
Christopher Pike's
*The Grave***

About the Author

CHRISTOPHER PIKE was born in Brooklyn, New York, but grew up in Los Angeles, where he lives to this day. Prior to becoming a writer, he worked in a factory, painted houses, and programmed computers. His hobbies include astronomy, meditating, running, playing with his nieces and nephews, and making sure his books are prominently displayed in local bookstores. He is the author of *Last Act, Spellbound, Gimme a Kiss, Remember Me, Scavenger Hunt, Final Friends* 1, 2, and 3, *Fall into Darkness, See You Later, Witch, Die Softly, Bury Me Deep, Whisper of Death, Chain Letter 2: The Ancient Evil, Master of Murder, Monster, Road to Nowhere, The Eternal Enemy, The Immortal, The Wicked Heart, The Midnight Club, The Last Vampire, The Last Vampire 2: Black Blood, The Last Vampire 3: Red Dice, Remember Me 2: The Return, Remember Me 3: The Last Story, The Lost Mind, The Visitor, The Last Vampire 4: Phantom, The Last Vampire 5: Evil Thirst, The Last Vampire 6: Creatures of Forever, Execution of Innocence, Tales of Terror #1, The Star Group, The Hollow Skull,* and *Tales of Terror #2,* all available from Archway Paperbacks. *Slumber Party, Weekend, Chain Letter,* and *Sati*—an adult novel about a very unusual lady—are also by Mr. Pike.

CHRISTOPHER PIKE'S

The Last Vampire

THE ANCIENT MONSTER.
THE MODERN HERO.

Collector's Edition, Vol. 1

INCLUDES
THE LAST VAMPIRE
THE LAST VAMPIRE 2: BLACK BLOOD
THE LAST VAMPIRE 3: RED DICE

Collector's Edition, Vol. 2

INCLUDES
THE LAST VAMPIRE 4: PHANTOM
THE LAST VAMPIRE 5: EVIL THIRST
THE LAST VAMPIRE 6: CREATURES OF FOREVER

From Archway Paperbacks
Published by Pocket Books

1472-01

Christopher Pike presents....
a frighteningly fun new series for your younger brothers and sisters!

SPOOKSVILLE™

A MINSTREL BOOK

"Well, we could grind our enemies into powder with a sledgehammer, but gosh, we did that last night."
— *XANDER*

BUFFY
THE VAMPIRE
SLAYER ™

As long as there have been vampires, there has been the Slayer. One girl in all the world, to find them where they gather and to stop the spread of their evil ... the swell of their numbers.

#1 THE HARVEST

#2 HALLOWEEN RAIN

#3 COYOTE MOON

#4 NIGHT OF THE LIVING RERUN

THE ANGEL CHRONICLES, VOL. 1

BLOODED

THE WATCHER'S GUIDE
(The Totally Pointy Guide for the Ultimate Fan!)

THE ANGEL CHRONICLES, VOL. 2

Based on the hit TV series created by Joss Whedon

 Published by Pocket Books